KEY

WEST

ESCAPE

A Tropical Adventure

Chuck Ball

An imprint of Road Trip Publishing

Advance Praise for **KEY WEST ESCAPE**:

An unconventional story teller, Chuck Ball took me away to the islands. His descriptions of tropical locales make me want to take a road trip. Key West is a character in his books that I feel I am getting to know. **KEY WEST ESCAPE** is a Margaritaville kind of story with an unexpected twist. Get out the flip flops and let's go.

-Dennis Rogers, author of
It's Bad News When the Bartender Cries,
Second Harvest and countless
columns for the News & Observer.

Chuck Ball continues to entertain us with tropical tales. **KEY WEST ESCAPE** is full of action, dialogue, quirky characters and well, the character Rainy. She is a hustler, stripper, artist, dominatrix, lesbian, feminist, heroine and philanthropist.

-Frank Amoroso, author of
Behind Every Great Fortune
and soon to be released *Dread the Fed.*

Bad guys, good guys, and the main character, Rainy...all woven into tropical heat, murder, gulf stream fishing, boat culture and the irreverent history of the Conch Republic. **KEY WEST ESCAPE** will capture you.

-Mike Hosick, author of
Skylarking and Other Pastimes

Also by Chuck Ball

Side Effects
Mingo's Cave
Hemingway's Heist

KEY WEST ESCAPE. Copyright 2015 by Chuck Ball.

For information:
Road Trip Publishing
246 Greenville Avenue
Wilmington, NC 28403

First Edition

Designed by Chuck Ball

ISBN: 1515023982

Dedication:

To Captain Morgan. Always good company

"Keys Disease is a severe plague on organized activities and the ability to move projects ahead at any rate of speed. In its most infectious state it is capable of totally destroying the concept of a deadline. Most susceptible to contamination are boaters, fisherman, sun bathers, lap swimmers, conch lovers and just about anyone who wanders below mile marker 126.5 on the Overseas Highway, also known as US 1 in farthest southeast reaches of the United States. The infection causes several days of euphoria and high excitement, followed by malaise and indifference to time commitments and obligations. Ocean breeze, intense sunshine, abundant fishing and a party atmosphere are thought to cause Keys Disease. Fortunately, since the disease is not fatal, periodic travel to the Keys is not physically or mentally life threatening and may, in fact, prolong life for those who expose themselves prudently."

From Lynnkipedia - a totally bogus free encyclopedia.

KEY WEST ESCAPE

Prologue

It was about three in the morning. Captain Freddy was in his bunk drunk. A random alcohol fueled neurological jolt boosted his subconscious to a level in which he felt someone step onto his boat. He struggled to get the clunky .38 Smith & Wesson out of the holster that hung on the hook by the door.

Freddy knew every creak of The Baron and figured someone was climbing up to the flybridge. He waited until the boat settled then crept out of the salon door. He crouched behind the fighting chair for cover.

Freddy used both hands to point the heavy gun. "Gonna blow your ass off my god damn boat!"

"Whoa! Freddy it's me, Roger. Don't shoot." A tall bald man stood with his hands in the air.

"That's a good way to get yourself fucked up. Didn't recognize you. What the hell?"

"Hey sorry, I had a chance to get away and didn't think to let you know." Roger slowly dropped his hands. "Not gonna shoot me are you?"

"Naw man ain't got no bullets." Freddy waved the gun around. "Stole this from my old man. He was a Detroit cop. C'mon down and have a drink."

Roger lugged his duffel bag down from the flybridge and dragged it into the salon.

"What 'cha want. Vodka? A shot?" Freddy put the gun on the counter and picked up a bottle.

"Yeah. What do ya say we take a few days and go over to Bimini?"

"Hell yeah man, ready to catch another big 'un!" Freddy wobbled around the salon. "Wanna leave now?"

"Let's do it. I'll get the lines."

So The Baron left Islamorada a couple of hours before any of the other charter boats would head out to fish.

Freddy got drunker. He gave up the wheel to Roger.

"Gonna go below. Wake me up when we're ready to fuckin' fish." Freddy disappeared down the ladder from the flybridge.

Roger watched the compass and headed toward Bimini. About two hours away from the mainland he put on the autopilot and climbed down to check on Freddy. He found him face down on the salon couch in a puddle of his own puke but still breathing.

Roger stepped out to the cockpit and looked around. It was dark. He didn't see running lights from any other boats. He went back into the salon, ignored the smell, and managed to get Freddy up on his feet.

"C'mon Freddy. Gonna put your ass in the fighting chair. Can you make it?"

"God damn right. Gonna catch a big mother. My turn."

Roger struggled to strap the fishing harness around Freddy. Then he clipped it to the big Penn reel and locked down the drag. This contraption hooked Freddy to the rod and reel but not the boat.

The Baron was moving at about trolling speed through calm seas. Roger busied himself with rigging the equipment. Freddy passed out in the chair.

"God damn Freddy! Set the hook!" Roger dropped a five gallon bucket attached to the fishing line over the stern. Freddy's head popped up off his chest and by reflex he hauled back. The rod bent into a 'C' and jerked him to his feet and over the transom.

Roger watched Freddy sputtering and floundering in The Baron's wake, the heavy rod and harness pulling him under.

A smile crossed his face as he climbed to the flybridge. He calmly pushed both throttles down.

Roger could have simply pushed Freddy off the boat. Using a bucket to pull him into the water was just way more satisfying.

Chapter 1

Redeeming qualities? Harvey never had any. When he
woke up in the morning his first thought was about himself.
Blame it on society if you want. Blame his poor parents but their
three other sons are fine people. Blame it on the school system.
Doesn't matter. Harvey inexplicably developed a sense that the
world should revolve around him alone. So early on, if he wanted
something he took it. If he was caught he lied. Punishment only
amused him. He kept his head down and promised to never do it
again. Of course he just became sneakier. Got away with more.
Minor thefts of pocket change grew into bigger amounts.

Cheating his way through high school got him a
scholarship to a top notch university. He was incredibly good
looking and charmed professors and fellow students. He was
considered an asset for the right fraternity and was rushed with
vigor. Somehow his fees were waived.

The fraternity had extensive test files and Harvey cheated
his way to a business degree. He didn't care about relationships
except to use them for his own benefit. The long line of frat
brothers led him to a job which gave him access to real money.
Guess you could say he was learning and applying his trade.

He began selling life insurance for a major New York
company. He discovered that he could easily manipulate his
clients. After he did the 'kitchen table' sales pitch that he called
'backing up the hearse', the young couple would be so distraught

they would sign anything. Often the new father's hand was shaking so much that Harvey would have to fill out the check for his signature.

An automatic monthly draft was set up from the account information on the check. The money was illegally deposited directly into Harvey's account. To cover his tracks about every third policy was legitimate with the checks going to the insurance company. The cash flowed in.

As long as none of the 'uninsured' died, Harvey could spend all the money on himself. A very simple and satisfying scam that caused Harvey no guilt.

Everyone in the small town of Frostville, North Carolina knew Harvey. As he matured he became even more attractive. Tall, physically fit with a neatly trimmed black beard and an engaging smile, his charisma inspired devotion.

Harvey advertised his business heavily. He piloted his own small plane and pulled a banner with his company's logo over any event in the county from tractor pulls to football games. He contributed to all the local causes. He coached Little League and was in church every Sunday. He had married up as they say. Harvey's wife Barbara's maiden name was Frost. She was descended from the wealthy founding family of the town. All part of the illusion that he was a solid citizen.

Sometimes in the early morning when he sat alone on his deck drinking coffee, Harvey did wonder how he could fake sincerity with such ease. What drove him to lie and steal? Why did he get such satisfaction when he got away with even the slightest deception, the meaner the better?

"He would steal money from his Mama" was a quote said about one of the local politicians. Harvey had even said it while that's exactly what he was doing. Ever the doting son, he made sure to 'tend' to his Mama when her Social Security check arrived. He stole about half of each deposit and siphoned off all her stock investments.

He even stole the passport from Dan Willis, his wife's dying cousin. He stole it not because he rationalized the only trip the man was going to take was to the great beyond, he stole it because he knew some day he would be on the run.

What was missing in him? Quickly he shook off those moments of self reflection and his feelings of entitlement resurfaced. He realized he only needed other people to get what he wanted.

Harvey partnered with a developer, who was also a cousin, to build a fancy gated subdivision called Oakmont. It was located just outside of the Research Triangle Park near Raleigh. A logical move for a prosperous young businessman.

The housing bubble was just beginning and his timing was perfect. This new scam was a little more complex. Harvey secured the construction loans for his cousin who built the houses. When a house was sold Harvey had devised a slick little deception. At the closing, his pretty secretary would 'walk' the mortgage company check to the bank. "Just as a service to save time so it won't have to be sent through the mail." She would explain with a sweet smile.

Instead of being deposited in escrow, as required by law, the check was deposited into Harvey's personal account. He never paid off the construction loan. As long as he paid the interest the bank that made the loan never knew. The homeowner wouldn't know there were two mortgages on the house until he tried to sell or borrow and two liens would show up. His cousin was not involved in the scam but would get the blame when it unraveled.

Now Harvey had some serious money.

Chapter 2

Smarter that most thieves, Harvey didn't rush out and buy a lot of bling or fast cars. His one indulgence was a used Cessna that he flew himself.

He had a nice but unpretentious house. Barbara was bugging him to move up to the country club neighborhood near her parents. He put her off but dangled such a move as a possibility.

He continued to coach and attend church. He also began taking 'business trips'. Explaining that he was attending insurance conferences or exploring possible real estate investments. He left the family behind for a week or so about once a month.

Harvey knew the insurance scam and the mortgage fraud would eventually be discovered. So he actively built a war chest of cash for his escape. The 'business trips' were officially to western North Carolina and Virginia, at least that's where his flight plan indicated. In reality he was going to the Florida Keys where he could land anonymously at any of a dozen rural airfields that for the right bribe would lose arrival and departure records.

There, Harvey became Roger and frequented the waterfront bars from Islamorada to Key West. He met a boat captain who became his drinking buddy.

Captain Freddy and Harvey, aka Roger, were an unlikely pair. Freddy was as tall as Roger but kind of mushy with long shaggy hair. The only exercise he got was bending his elbow with shots of vodka. He owned a fishing boat named The Baron. He kept it in an Islamorada marina. As far as Roger could tell the boat was Freddy's home that he sometimes shared with a woman named Rainy.

Rainy was a tall woman with a tattoo of her own profile on her shoulder. She liked to wear micro bikinis and long wigs. Her body did not betray her age. Only her frown lines made it obvious she was closer to forty than thirty. She was beautiful and oozed sexual mischief. Men and women were hooked by her sensual package and raucous laugh.

She made her living as an airbrush artist and dominatrix, working up and down the Keys. She mostly painted bodies of conservative, overweight Midwestern white women and slapped around their husbands. They came to the Florida Keys for a titillating vacation and to attend weird clothing optional festivals such as Fantasy Fest in Key West. Rainy knew how to seduce as she painted their bloated bodies. The women felt an erotic charge as she whispered suggestively and lightly touched them. The men ached for her to dominate them. They always left sizable tips.

She and Freddy were not exactly a couple. Roger figured they had scammed plenty of people and had a relationship of convenience. Rainy always seemed to be on the run from suckers she ripped off or more serious criminals she had tangled with. She did occasionally join in on some of their bar hopping nights. Sometimes she flirted with Roger and made it clear she was available for a price. He was interested, but too conservative to cross over to the dark side.

Captain Freddy and Roger trolled for mackerel and wahoo on The Baron and drank at the dockside bars. At first, Roger really didn't care much about fishing. He was just looking to build trust with someone who knew about boats and was a little shady. It was part of his exit strategy.

On these excursions Roger was always careful to use sunscreen and keep covered to prevent sunburn. He didn't want to come home to Frostville from his 'business trip' looking like he had been lying on a beach somewhere. He dropped his 'fishy' clothes at a dry cleaner near the marina and they held them until he returned. It didn't seem like an unusual request particularly since Roger tipped so well.

Harvey, aka Roger, kept a storage unit near the General Aviation airport outside of Raleigh and had another unit in Asheville. He slowly filled both with cash. He was careful to make modest bank withdrawals to avoid suspicion. He paid cash for everything on his 'business trips' so he wouldn't leave an electronic trail. He took care of the household bills so his busy wife never knew exactly what their financial situation was. Barbara didn't care as long as she had money to spend.

On each trip to Florida, Harvey also took a duffel bag of cash and hid it on The Baron. Captain Freddy didn't ask questions because Roger paid for his silence and was his only customer.

Chapter 3

Harvey decided it was time to amp up the cash flow. Holding back interest payments and just dragging his feet with excuses to the bank could add millions of dollars to his Fuck You (FU) money. That, plus the amount he had already stolen would give him enough to put his plan into effect.

The Oakmont development near Raleigh was about an hour and a half away from Frostville. No one from the local bank ever bothered to visit the site because the interest payments were always made on time. The people who worked at the Bank of Frostville trusted Harvey so the first week the interest payment was late he received a polite reminder by email from a bank clerk. Harvey ignored it and went on a 'business trip' and hauled more cash to Florida.

When he got to Islamorada he asked Captain Freddy if they could go for some trophy fish. He said he was tired of messing around with table fare. Captain Freddy was thrilled to take his best and only customer out after marlin. Rainy had no interest so she took off for Key West to make some money.

It took a half day to provision The Baron to be able to venture across the Gulf Stream. They would fish in the fabled big game waters off Bimini then return to Islamorada.

Roger used the passport he had stolen from his wife's dead cousin so he could enter the Bahamas. He even paid for a new navigation system and charts to make sure they could find their way over and back.

Freddy had crossed the Gulf Stream to fish near Bimini a few times as a mate on other boats and had piloted The Baron across once. This would be his first fishing trip as captain. He was nervous and excited. He knew to leave at daybreak to catch the Stream in a calm mood. If the wind was North West the seas could be very difficult. Fortunately when they left the dock, there was barely a breeze. He pushed the twin throttles down and the 38 footer planed easily in the light chop. Bimini was about 100 miles from Islamorada. The best marlin water was about half way. Roger studied the charts and asked Freddy lots of questions about the water and islands and cays around Bimini.

After hours of trolling they finally had a strike. A skipping ballyhoo was attacked and the fish pulled the line from the outrigger clip. Freddy yelled at Roger to set the hook. He did and the heavy trolling rod bent into a 'C' and almost took him overboard. When he got his feet planted in the fighting chair, the fish stripped hundreds of feet of line and went deep. Captain Freddy shouted for Roger to keep the rod tip up and he tried to maneuver the boat to run with the unseen fish. The fight lasted only about five minutes before the hook pulled.

Hours later when The Baron was back at the Islamorada dock, Roger and Captain Freddy were still pumped full of adrenaline. The trip had been an adventure. They were both eager to try again. Roger said he would be back soon for a second attempt.

Chapter 4

When Harvey got back to Frostville he had a couple of voicemails from a bank vice president politely asking for a meeting. He returned the call and a meeting was set for that Friday.

Harvey skipped the meeting, morphed into Roger and again left town. This time he and Captain Freddy spent three days fishing. Each night they pulled into the Anchorage Marina on Bimini and slept on the boat which had two cabins. They had raised and hooked three marlin but had not boated one. In the marina bar Roger bought the old salts plenty of drinks and got sage advice about what they were doing wrong.

On the third day Captain Freddy and Roger trolled back toward Islamorada. About halfway across the Gulf Stream a marlin came up into the skipping baits. Roger now knew how to drop the ballyhoo back to make it look wounded. When he did the fish hit it and Roger set the hook by pumping the rod hard three times. The battle was on.

Roger settled into the fighting chair. With just two on board The Baron, landing a big marlin would be a challenge. The 38 foot boat was smaller than most used for this kind of fishing but it was fast and nimble which could help. The big fish headed west as if it didn't know it was hooked. Roger pumped the rod and reeled. He gained some line then lost it. Remembering what some of the fishermen in Bimini had told him, he tried to keep the rod tip high and the line tight. Slack line was the reason most fish got away.

The fish jumped and tail-walked trying to throw the hook it now felt. It was 'lit up' as the old timers would say. Its body an iridescent blue. Roger hauled in line as Freddy closed the distance to the frantic fish. Each time Roger reeled and pumped the fish got closer to the transom. Then it would spook and take off on another long run.

Captain Freddy tried to keep pace. Roger was tiring. The battle had lasted over an hour now and the hot tropical sun was taking a toll.

"Cut the fucking line Roger." Freddy yelled down from the flybridge. "You gonna have a heat stroke."

"I'm okay. Okay. Just back down."

Freddy put the boat in reverse. The idea was to get back some of the line. Waves crashed over the transom and the foaming water slid around the cockpit and out the scuppers. The cool water actually revived Roger and he pumped the rod and reeled with renewed vigor. The fish seemed to have turned toward the boat.

"Think you're gaining on him." Freddy was twisted around in the captain's chair to see where he was steering. Roger pumped and reeled faster as the boat slammed backward into the waves. Then the fish sounded.

"Stop Freddy!" On the flybridge Freddy pulled the twin throttles into neutral and The Baron drifted. "He's under the boat and going down!"

Freddy bumped the throttles forward to change the angle of the line. Then he climbed down to the cockpit. He got two bottles of water from the cooler. He poured one over Roger and gave him one to drink.

"That is a monster fish Roger, he could stay down for a long time. If you're gonna keep fighting him you need to drink a lot of water." Roger just nodded and drank most of the bottle of water in one gulp.

"He doesn't seem to be moving." Roger lifted the rod tentatively.

"Resting. Think he will come up soon. Just be ready to reel."

Roger laid back against the fighting chair to relieve his back. "Man, I'm gonna be sore tomorrow."

"Yeah you are."

Freddy sat on the transom and looked down at the line. He was worried that a shark would attack the marlin since it was tired and probably bleeding some from its gills. He hoped the fish would start to move soon.

"Hey Freddy I can feel him. Like he's shaking his head."

"Probably is. Hang on" Freddy climbed back up to the flybridge. He could see how dark the water was and knew they were probably in the middle of the Gulf Stream and about half way back to Islamorada. He was getting a little concerned about how much fuel he had left.

"He's moving." Roger yelled. He leaned forward and pumped the rod. "He's coming up!"

"Keep pumping man, keep pumping!" Freddy put the throttle into forward gear just as the fish exploded through the surface of the dark ocean. It was only about ten yards behind the boat. Water streamed off the big fish as it hung for a few seconds eying its adversary then crashed into frothy wake of the boat.

"Holy shit! Its huge!" Roger was stunned.

"Pump and reel! Pump and reel!" Freddy put the engines in neutral and came off the flybridge. He grabbed a long handled gaff and leaned over the transom. "I can see the leader. Keep reeling." The fish went down again but not so deep. Roger pumped the rod and started to get back the line.

"Okay ease off. Let me get the leader." Freddy put on gloves and pulled the double line toward the boat. "Roger, unhook the harness from the reel and come help me."

When Roger got out of the fighting chair he could barely stand. His legs were cramping.

"Take the gaff. When I get him close, slam it into his back as hard as you can. Then hang on!"

The big fish floated up on its side just beyond the reach of the gaff. Freddy gently pulled on the leader guiding the animal closer to the boat.

"Okay Roger, hit him!

Roger leaned out and the long handled gaff whooshed toward the fish. He missed. He was short. Freddy dropped the leader just as the startled fish rolled under the water with one sweep of its tail.

"God damn it Roger. Get back in the chair."

The fish dove again. Roger pumped the rod and soon the leader reappeared. Freddy once again got hold of the double line.

"Okay Roger, this time I'll get him closer. But don't fucking miss again!"

Freddy pulled the fish slowly toward the boat. Roger stood by ready with the gaff. The fish was now defeated. It lolled on its side in the trough of the waves, its big eye the size of a dinner plate stared at the sky. This time when the gaff whooshed through the air it struck hard into the shoulder muscle. The fish jolted a bit but was done. Freddy got a tail rope on it and cleated it to the transom.

Roger sagged down onto the cockpit sole exhausted. Freddy sat on the gunwale and stared down at the huge fish.

"Eh, Freddy what do we do now?" Roger looked up as sweat dried on his face.

Freddy knew what he meant. There was no way the two of them could pull the fish into the boat. It was about dead and if they cut it loose it would just be shark food. He looked around hoping to see another boat. A bigger one that might have block and tackle and a post for hauling in a big fish. There were none in sight and even if he hailed another boat on the radio, the sharks would destroy the fish before it arrived.

"If we can get the tail up over the transom without sinking us, I think I can get a few wraps around the anchor windlass and winch it in." Freddy opened a locker and began tying a heavy line to the tail rope.

"Worth a shot, I guess." Together they managed to get the heavy fish turned and dragged the tail up onto the transom. Freddy ran the line through the cabin and out the bow hatch. He wrapped it around the windlass.

"I'm gonna start the winch. Just pull as hard as you can."

The line tightened as Freddy got a wrap around the winch and then another. The motor was designed to retrieve a hundred pound anchor and Freddy was worried it would quickly burn out. He got another wrap on it as Roger pulled the line in the cockpit. Slowly the big fish came aboard. Its weight almost pushed the transom below the water, but finally most of the animal was in the boat.

"How much do you think it weighs?" Roger was kneeling.

"Not a clue but we need to keep it wet on the trip in. I'm gonna get some sheets and towels to wrap it up. You put a line on that bait bucket to douse it as we go."

"Why go to all that trouble?" Roger touched the fish as its colors faded.

"Could be a fucking record so don't want it to dry out and lose weight."

"A record?" Roger looked astounded.

"Could be, it's a big mother." Freddy couldn't help himself. He quoted a famous line from Captain Quint in Jaws. *"Back home we got a taxidermy man. He gonna have a heart attack when he see what I brung him."*

Captain Freddy knew from his GPS that he was about half way across the Gulf Stream. He thought about where a big fish like this could possibly be a record. If he went back to Bimini he was pretty sure there had been bigger ones weighed in at the Anchorage Marina. So he decided to motor on to Islamorada hoping for at least a local record. He had never brought in a marlin so he had always been ignored by the 'real' charter captains. This fish would change his status in the cliquey community.

Roger sat in the shade of the flybridge and looked down at the fish. He had never had an adventure like this. It was too bad he couldn't ever let anyone back home know about it. If he revealed he had been in the Florida Keys he would blow the escape route that he had so meticulously planned.

"Hey Roger." Freddy had to raise his voice over the wind noise on the flybridge. "Go below and look in the locker under the chart table. There should be a marlin pennant in a new package on the top shelf. Break it out and run it up the outrigger." Freddy smiled.

"New you say?" Roger laughed.

"Yeah, never caught one but always hoped to."

Roger found the pennant and ran it up the outrigger. It was a sign to the other fisherman that the boat had caught a marlin.

About a half hour out, Freddy radioed the marina to let them know he would be off loading a fish and that he would need the Harbor Master to do the official weigh in. This message stirred some excitement among the dock watchers. Freddy had never called in before so they knew he must have something big. The word zipped around the close-knit fishing community and people started gathering at the dock.

When Freddy came down the narrow channel to the marina he could see people waiting. He was nervous and excited. Just one slip up while docking The Baron would be embarrassing. He carefully tractored the boat around and slowly backed into the slip. The crowd caught sight of the fish. An excited murmur spread through the usually unimpressed old salts.

Roger stood at the stern and caught the dock lines. He cleated them off and then went forward and rigged the bow lines.

"God damn Freddy! You got yourself a big 'un there," one of the crusty old captains yelled and the crowd laughed. Freddy basked in the attention as he went through the process of unloading the fish.

Roger and Freddy pulled the line that ran through the heavy block and tackle attached to the giant scale hanging from a cross beam on the dock. A local jumped into the boat to help. As the fish lifted off the cockpit sole the audience got a good look. The murmurs turned to awe.

Once the fish was swinging free the Harbor Master who officially represented the International Game Fish Association stepped up to check the weight.

"One thousand sixty-one." He called out. "One thousand sixty-one pounds." He wrote the number on a form attached to the clipboard he was carrying then painted it on the side of the fish.

Freddy and Roger looked satisfied. "Big damn fish!" One of the charter captains commented. "Might near a record."

The Harbor Master looked up. "Might near? Hell, it is the Florida record. Beats the old one of one thousand forty six pounds."

Spontaneous applause broke out and people started taking pictures with their iPhones. A reporter from the Keys News pushed through the crowd and posed Freddy and Roger in front of the fish for a shot.

At the last second Roger snatched a long billed hat off of a spectator and jammed it down on his head to try to cover his face. The reporter took the shot. Roger didn't want anyone to recognize him back home in case the story of the record fish went viral.

Chapter 5

The next day Roger flew back to North Carolina. The feeling of excitement about his adventure with Freddy was unexpected and a bit puzzling. He rarely felt passion for anything.

Now he had to make the mental switch to dealing with the bank and the late payment on his loans. He had only talked to his wife once since he left because he rarely turned his cell phone on.

When he checked his voicemail, it was full. Most of the messages were from the bank and predictable. First there was a polite inquiry about why he missed the meeting with the bank VP. Then the messages got more demanding. Harvey skipped most of them. The last one was from Barbara and she sounded stressed. Evidently the bank had sent someone to their house looking for Harvey. She didn't know anything about the family finances. He decided to just wait until he was back in NC before he called her, being mindful that cell phone transmissions could be tracked.

Harvey flicked on his cell phone once he had driven out of the General Aviation airport near Raleigh. Immediately it rang. He saw it was Barbara and answered. She was angry and crying. She didn't know why the bank was harassing her and why Harvey had not returned her calls. He simply lied and said he had broken his phone. Then, he calmed her down by saying the bank had made a mistake and it would be cleared up as soon as he got home.

The drive from the airport took about an hour and a half. Harvey decided his schemes were unraveling and it was time to flee. He had a carefully laid out a plan that involved his plane and a car in his storage unit in Asheville. First he needed to go home to throw his wife and the bank off his trail.

The next morning Harvey carefully dressed in his best charcoal grey suit. He would take full advantage of his good looks and charm. Earlier he had eased his wife's concerns. She had headed out to drop the kids at school and go to her woman's club meeting. Now he would visit the Bank of Frostville and calm down the Vice President who was about to stroke out over the late payment. He knew just what to say. He had to present an opportunity for the bank to make more money. As he tied his silk tie he mentally rehearsed.

Later as he sat at his office desk he smiled. The meeting with the bank official went just as expected. He explained the bare details of a big development deal in Asheville. That was why the interest payment on Oakmont was late. He had used the cash for earnest money. The new deal had to be kept secret until it closed. He manipulated the banker's greed and the trust he had built over many years. Now he had bought time to escape.

Harvey was the loving husband and family man for a week while he methodically destroyed his office files and dismantled the computers. Then he told his wife he was off to close the biggest deal of his life and when he did she could pick out a new 'Country Club' house.

Harvey kept his Cessna 172 at the general aviation airport connected to the Raleigh Durham Airport. He loaded up a duffel bag from his storage unit and easily took it through the terminal security as he had done many times before and put it on his plane. He had filed a flight plan to the Asheville Regional Airport. The trip was uneventful and he left the plane in a rented hangar. It was a quick cab ride into town to a Holiday Inn. He checked in, put his overnight bag in room 202, then took the duffel bag, slipped down the stairs and out the back of the building. He was sure no one saw him leave. It took only a few minutes for him to walk to the long term storage unit and a stolen used car. He loaded up more of the cash he had stored but left behind a substantial reserve in ten attache cases. He attached pilfered license tags and soon was on the road heading south. Harvey figured it would take him about twelve hours to get to Islamorada.

Chapter 6

The bank VP that Harvey had charmed was again nervous. He had not gotten many details about the 'big deal' Harvey said he was about to close. Now the bank's auditor was asking about a shortfall of millions of dollars in the Oakmont account. He tried to reach Harvey with no success so he called Barbara. She arrogantly reassured the worried executive by telling him that Harvey was always reliable. She felt sure he would hear about the deal in the next few days. The bank VP was still worried but figured he had no choice but to wait for Harvey's call. It never came.

WRAL the local CBS affiliate broke the story.

A prominent eastern NC businessman is missing. Harvey Hall is described as an integral member of the Frostville community. His wife, Barbara stated that he often took business trips in his own airplane. This time she had not heard from him since he left five days ago. She reported him missing.

Immediate speculation was that he may have crashed in the mountains but his airplane, a Cessna 172 with the tail number N78253 has been found at a general aviation airport near Asheville. The destination he filed on his flight plan. It was determined that he took a cab to town and

*checked into the Holiday Inn on June 26. His overnight bag
was found. Then the trail has gone cold.*

*Authorities are requesting help in finding Harvey
Hall. He is forty two years old, six feet two inches tall,
weighs 175 pounds with blue eyes, black hair and a full
beard. He is from Frostville, North Carolina. If you have
any information about Harvey Hall contact your local
police.*

Speculation about Harvey's disappearance was all anyone
was talking about around Frostville. When it was discovered that
Harvey had traveled to Asheville to close a big deal many
suspected foul play. The popular theory was that he had a large
amount of cash and someone killed him for it.

The bank VP suspected something different, particularly
when the auditor found even more money misdirected from
Oakmont development to Harvey's personal account. The
amount was more than fifteen million dollars. His boss did not
want to go to the authorities because it would expose the banks'
lax oversight of favored customers. There were all kinds of
ramifications to this kind of fiscal malfeasance. The most
important was the VP and his boss being fired. So initially the
loss was covered up.

In the meantime Harvey's wife, Barbara, was discovering
that she was broke. She had never paid any attention to money,
except to spend it. Now the bank told her the checking and
saving accounts were empty. Not a penny. She panicked. Fear for
her husband's life turned to anger. Her whole perfect life was
disappearing. How was it possible that there was no money?

Harvey always said they had plenty and she would never have to worry.

The police in Frostville were stymied. The cops in Asheville were not very helpful because the 'missing man' was not a local and as far as they were concerned could have just run off with his mistress. There was no evidence to suggest otherwise. The hotel room was unused. The airplane was spotless.

Chapter 7

With callous disregard for his family and his clients Harvey drove on. He found a good rock & roll radio station and cranked it up. When 'Born to be Wild' came on he sang every word at the top of his lungs. He had plenty of cash and had left no trail. No one would find him. All the painstaking planning was working out. He stopped for more coffee then drove on.

In Frostville, more rumors began to fly around after one of Harvey's insurance clients died. The family filed a death certificate with the New York company that supposedly issued the policy on the man's life only to discover that it had no record of any premium payments ever being made. The detective that was handling the missing person case on Harvey also listened to the confused angry family of the recently deceased man. He called in the State Bureau of Investigation because now there seemed to be evidence of fraud as well as a missing person.

A team of computer and forensic specialists searched Harvey's office. They found nothing. The seasoned investigators reported to their supervisor that they had never seen a room so totally devoid of any possible evidence. Not only had the place been chemically cleaned but the computers contained no hard drives or any recoverable files. There weren't even any customer contacts. The suspicion of multiple crimes intensified as a result. What was emerging was a well planned theft and escape. The SBI could only dig deeper by old fashion police work. Investigators fanned out through Frostville to ask people if they had ever done business with Harvey. It was soon discovered that most had.

More people dug out their life insurance policies as word of Harvey's deception spread. Many discovered that the automatic monthly bank drafts on their statements had not paid the premiums. In fact, in those cases there never was a real policy issued, only a certificate from Harvey that turned out to be bogus. Now the FBI was called in because the so-called insurance company policies Harvey was selling were from out of state. The case had become more complex.

Chapter 8

Barbara Hall was desperate. She had been to the Frostville Bank which ironically had been started by her great grandfather. She confirmed Harvey had drained the accounts. Even her safety deposit box which had held savings bonds was empty except for a single key. She had no idea what it was for but she put it in her purse.

She spoke to a loan officer to try to borrow against the equity of their house only to discover a Home Equity Line of Credit (HELOC) had already been used and the payment was late. Now the bank could take the house. Outside she sat in her car and cried. Why would Harvey do this to her and his children? How could he be so mean? What was she going to do?

Across town in a rented store front the Joint Interagency Task Force (JITF) was meeting. The Frostville police chief, the SBI, the FBI, a representative from the State Attorney's office and the Director of Security from the New York insurance company were trying to figure out how much money Harvey had stolen and even more important where he might be. More information from the bank suggested that as much as fifteen million dollars was stolen from Oakmont development. The amount stolen in the insurance fraud was almost impossible to calculate since it had taken place over many years. The Director of Security said the number could be five million or higher. He could only make an estimate based on the number of people who had already stepped forward with bogus policies.

The debate about where Harvey might be was endless. It seemed the man had disappeared like 'a fart in the wind' according to the Frostville Police Chief, Wilbur Bonnet who also was an owner of a bogus insurance policy.

At the Bank of Frostville the Vice President and his boss huddled to decide if they could keep the cover up of the construction loans and mortgage fraud going. They both knew that it was only a matter of time before one of Oakmont homeowners tried to sell and the deception would be discovered. The two men plotted to throw Harvey and his cousin under the bus to try to avoid their complicity.

Even as they concocted a story to do this, the fraud was surfacing. A couple, one of the first buyers in Oakmont development, discovered as they tried to close the sale of their house that there were two liens, a construction loan and a mortgage loan. Their lawyer took the evidence to the SBI and the scheme was revealed. Harvey's cousin was arrested.

Harvey pulled into a rest stop off of I-95 somewhere in Georgia. He took his shaving kit into the bathroom and got rid of the beard he had worn for most of his adult life. He shaved his head. It was a dramatic change to his appearance. He was thrilled. He got another cup of vending machine coffee and drove on. He figured if he could remain free for another couple of days he could disappear forever.

Chapter 9

After killing Freddy, Roger and The Baron motored on. As the sun rose, he calculated in his head a rough number for how much cash he had stashed on the boat. He knew a cubic foot of one hundred dollar bills was roughly one million dollars and weighed about 22 pounds. He thought he had about ten cubic feet stored on The Baron and at least that much in the storage unit back in North Carolina. So he had around about twenty million dollars in cash. Should be enough to live comfortably in the Bahamas for the rest of his life.

He had thoroughly studied the charts of the area and after he presented his stolen passport for entrance to Bimini, he knew exactly which one of the hundreds of islands he wanted to land on. It was remote in that there was no cell phone coverage and US news was irrelevant. He figured no one would miss Freddy.

Roger would have time to get rid of The Baron and Captain Freddy's meager possessions. Then he would buy a bigger boat.

He was enjoying the solitude of the flybridge in the early morning air as The Baron cut easily through the light chop.

"What the fuck?" Roger was so startled to hear a voice he turned the steering wheel sharply to port as he whirled around in the captain's chair.

Rainy, dressed in only the brief bottom of a tiny bikini stumbled and managed to fall onto the settee on the flybridge and not go overboard. Roger righted the boat and backed the throttles down.

"Where the hell are we?" Rainy stood and held her hand over her eyes like a busty figurehead on the prow of a pirate ship. "Where the hell is Freddy? He never told me we were going on a god damn trip."

"Damn Rainy, I didn't even know you were on board." Roger grimaced. "Going to Bimini."

"Me and Freddy had a god damn large night. Then got to fuckin' arguing and I locked myself in the guest cabin. Passed out, I guess." She tried to smile but it was an effort. "Gotta get some coffee. That crazy Freddy, bet he's still the fuck asleep."

"Deeply, I would guess." Roger's mind was reeling.

"Gonna make coffee. Want some?" Rainy clearly knew she was offering more than coffee. She was over Freddy and figured this good looking square civilian might be a better gig.

"Sure, I want some." Roger got the message. "Let Freddy sleep it off."

Now Roger thought he would have to kill Rainy too. His first thought was to just pitch her overboard. But as he looked around he could see a fair number of boats nearby. He didn't want to take the chance that some bored fisherman might be scanning with binoculars and spot a half naked girl going over the side. He had to come up with another plan. At the moment though he would just let things play out. Rainy assumed Freddy was unconscious in the Owner's cabin so that would buy some time.

When Rainy came back up to the flybridge she had put on a tank top. The tattoo of her profile on her shoulder peeked out almost like a bruise. She had a thermos and two mugs.

"Drink it black, don't 'cha?" She poured a mug and handed it to Roger with a smile. "Like this new look on you." She caressed his bald head. "I feel like fuckin' shit. Got all sweaty in that cabin, but it is nice up here with this breeze." She fluffed her skimpy shirt to fan herself.

Roger took a sip, conscious that this was as nice as Rainy had ever been to him. He began to think she might be open to a new arrangement without Freddy.

"What'd you two fight about?" Roger asked.

"Dumb ass stuff. Nothing really. Just stupid drunk shit." Rainy brought the thermos over to the pilot chair and leaned across Roger to refill his mug.

She had a hot musky kind of smell. She exuded danger and sexuality. So exotic when compared to his woman's club missionary position wife. He decided right then he had to make her part of his crew. The question was would she go for it?

"You two been together for a long time." It was more of a statement than a question. Roger was just sizing her up.

"Too fuckin' long." Rainy gazed toward the horizon. "Time for a change."

"Hey I get it. I'm doing that myself."

"What?"

Roger decided to reveal some of his plan to get a reaction. He still might have to kill her but maybe she could work into his cover. After all the law would be looking for him by himself. He had no history of running around with women. Not even his wife would believe he had taken up with trailer trash like Rainy.

41

"Just dumping my old life and starting fresh." Roger smiled. He knew he was extremely good looking and even as jaded as Rainy was about men she probably was attracted to him.

"What was your old life? I don't even fuckin' know where you come from?" Rainy tied the t-shirt around her waist so that her firm abs were visible above her bikini line.

"Not important. Just tired of that old life. Want to live in the sun."

"You're running. I know about running. Kill some poor fucker?" Her hazel eyes lit up with interest. She could identify with this need.

"Would you care?" Roger challenged.

Rainy laughed. "Naw. Was it Freddy?

Roger shrugged.

"You rich?" Rainy was totally interested.

"I am, you in?"

Rainy had made impulsive decisions all her life usually with disastrous results. She nodded.

"What about Freddy?" Roger asked.

"Fuck him."

"You sure about that?"

"Hell yeah."

"All right then. It's you and me."

Rainy didn't want to know more. She leaned around Roger and kissed him deeply. He tasted the salty dried sweat on her neck. She pulled off her tank top and swung a leg over his lap. Roger put the boat on autopilot as they consummated their unlikely alliance.

Chapter 10

Roger entered the Bahamas in Bimini with the stolen passport of Dan Willis from Danville, Virginia and Rainy hidden in the engine room. He topped off the fuel tanks on The Baron and motored on to Harbor Island near Eleuthera. He checked in with the harbormaster and rented a long term slip in the marina.

In the next few weeks Roger and Rainy drank in the sea side bars, had coffee in the local shop. Rainy took full advantage of the resort spa. Soon people didn't even see them anymore. They had become just one more attractive couple on a boat. Rainy never said another word about Freddy.

As Roger expected there were plenty of boats for sale and he spent a lot of time talking to owners and crew members of vessels that were bigger and more comfortable than The Baron. He made an offer of $300,000 cash on a 54' Bertram Sportfisher. The owner accepted and threw in plenty of fishing gear.

Soon Roger and Rainy cleaned out The Baron. They moved to the new boat he named Catch'Em with a little ironic nod to fishing and law enforcement.

Once they settled in he put a For Sale sign on The Baron. The tricky part was that he had no documents since he had stolen the boat from Captain Freddy after he killed him. But Roger figured he could find a shady buyer if he priced it low enough. He was right and soon a guy brought him cash and asked no questions. The Baron disappeared. Roger felt there was nothing left to link him to Freddy or his crimes in the States, except Rainy.

Roger's new boat was much more comfortable and better equipped than The Baron. Rainy put her stuff in the locker in one of the guest berths. They spent most nights in the owner's cabin together but they both needed their own space.

Even with dramatically different backgrounds they were very compatible initially. Mostly they just wanted to hang out in the sun, drink and fuck. Roger had added fishing to the list. Rainy thought that was boring.

Catching the record breaking marlin with Freddy had ignited fishing fever and meeting Rainy had ignited kinky passion. Roger had never experienced either. Now he had the right boat to chase monster fish and the right woman to satisfy his increasingly bizarre sexual appetite.

One problem was that he didn't want to keep his cash on the boat while he fished. So he quietly looked around for a cottage with a boat slip and pier. One of his new drinking buddies told him about a house that was for sale or rent in Spanish Wells and it had a deep water slip.

Spanish Wells is a small town on the tiny island of St. George's Cay. About two miles long and a half mile wide. Roger left Rainy sunbathing in the nude on the new boat and took the short ferry ride over from Harbor Island to explore. He rented a golf cart, the island's main mode of transportation and rode off down South Street to look for the house he had heard about.

He found the neatly kept cottage with the boat slip across the street. A 'For Sale or Rent' sign was in the yard. There was no number to call but instructions to inquire about the house at the

Ice Cream Shop. Roger asked a passerby for directions and quickly found the shop. Inside a pretty woman offered a friendly greeting. She asked him if he would like to try the shop specialty called 'the kitchen sink'. Roger smiled and nodded. Soon he was charming her and getting the background on Spanish Wells as well as learning about the cottage. Apparently the current owner lived in the States and rarely used the property. She gave him the name of a local attorney who could handle the deal.

Roger found the attorney's office and made a cash offer to rent for six months with an option to buy without ever entering the cottage. The attorney didn't ask too many questions and filed the contract into a newly created LLC for Roger. As improbable as this transaction may seem it was not that unusual in the islands where most deals are made with cash and sources are not questioned. Once again Roger and Rainy moved.

The new place had a workshop out back. Roger discovered a trap door in the floor. It led down to a ten by ten foot room that held empty storage racks. He immediately thought this would be a good place to hide his cash. However he needed to know more about the history of the house. This hidden room might be common knowledge on the island. He also needed to keep the cash and the hiding spot a secret from Rainy. He was happy to share his boat, cottage and bed but not all his money.

Roger began to frequent the Little Bar, the local hangout in Spanish Wells. It was a guy thing so he left Rainy at home. She didn't care. She began spending a lot of time painting. She had some talent but had squandered it to paint bodies instead of canvas. Now that she didn't have to scrape for a living she set up a studio in the workshop. Without knowing it she placed her easel right over the hidden storage room. Roger thought this just added to his cover. If anyone asked, they came to the island to fish and paint.

In the Little Bar he bought more than his share of rounds and was soon one of guys. Slowly he solicited information about the cottage he had rented. He learned that it was quite old, being built in the 1700's by one of the island's original settlers. 'Adventurers' they were called. It was known as the Sanderson house by the old timers but nowadays it is the Pineapple House. So called because the second owner made a business out of selling carved pineapple finials. At least that was some of the story. There were also some confusing episodes about the owner and stolen gold and murder. Roger had a hard time following the drunk fishermen who were trying to remember the details.

At no time had the hidden room come up in all the drunk ramblings so Roger felt it was not a well known tidbit about the cottage. He decided it was a safe place for his cash. After he moved it off his new boat he planned to do some fishing.

Chapter 11

For months the JITF sifted through tips and leads as to Harvey's where abouts. It had become a game of 'Where's Harvey?' as he was falsely spotted all over the US and as far away as Brazil. The case remained open but eventually the Joint Interagency Task Force was disbanded.

The Oakmont development went into bankruptcy when it was discovered all the homes had two loans against them. Harvey's cousin continued to proclaim his innocence. His trial was set for early Spring.

The squabbling bank and mortgage company could not decide how to resolve the mess. Lawsuits were filed.

Harvey's insurance clients including the police chief were out of pocket the money that for years had been automatically drafted from their checking accounts to pay for phantom insurance policies. The 'policy holders' complained to the insurance company named on the bogus certificates because Harvey was their agent. The company took no responsibility for his fraudulent activity. A lawsuit was filed.

The Frostville Bank Vice President and his boss were fired. Oakmont homeowners blamed them for slack oversight. A lawsuit was filed.

Barbara Hall lost her home to the bank. She maintained that Harvey forged her signature on HELOC documents. A lawsuit was filed.

The chaos Harvey left behind was worsening. Barbara and her children had to move in with her parents. The Oakmont development was becoming a shabby ghost town as more of the home owners walked away from properties they couldn't sell or pay for. The bank that made the construction loans to Harvey was bought by a larger one, but the lawsuits remained unsettled.

The law enforcement agencies that were involved put Harvey's picture and story on 'America's Most Wanted' but his trail remained cold.

Anyone that thought about Captain Freddy at all figured he had just drifted further down the Keys as so many of the transient population in Florida ultimately did.

The only person with even the slightest interest in his whereabouts was the marina owner because Freddy was past due on his slip rental bill. Of course even this wasn't too unusual and he figured he would just rent the empty slip to the next wandering captain that showed up.

So apparently Harvey Hall had committed the perfect crime.

Chapter 12

The foundation of Roger and Rainy's new relationship, R & R they called it, was booze and sex. For months Roger put Rainy on a pedestal. He showered her with gifts and she role played any sexual fantasy he could come up with. He liked that she had a long lean slick body that she pampered with exotic scents and full Brazilians from the spa. She teased him in public by touching him surreptitiously. She made him watch her flirt with the women that came off the visiting yachts. She would drive him close to climax only to completely push him away and ignore his pleas. She dominated him physically and played mind games that he found frustrating and exciting.

In the workshop studio she transferred her skill of painting bodies of women for festivals to painting female nudes on canvas. She found willing models everywhere. Mostly bored women off the expensive fishing machines that docked on Harbor Island.

She lined the workshop studio with erotic art and pictures. She was as skilled at capturing the beauty of her subjects as she was at seducing them.

Rainy liked to take the taxi boat over to Harbor Island and have coffee at the wharfside shop. There she could watch the women poke around in the tiny shops while their men were off doing their macho fishing thing. Inevitably she would start up a conversation with the most striking shopper and buy her a cup of coffee. Rainy would explain that she was an artist, then offer to paint her portrait ostensibly as a surprise for her captain. Very rarely would a woman turn her down.

Rainy may have come from trailer trash but she had learned to take advantage of her lean fit body. She had pronounced hip bones that she emphasized with tiny micro bikinis and firm abs. She glided when she moved, elegantly dressed in sexy beach casual wear with lots of contemporary jewelry. She mirrored the snotty rich women from the yachts. She made sure the portrait tattoo of her face with pouty lips did peek out of her bikini cover up. The yachty women found this very exciting. The possibility of spending time alone with Rainy was risky enough to be a turn on for even these world weary travelers.

Though Rainy's body language oozed seductiveness, she was subtle as she lightly touched the 'model' on her back and guided her to the water taxi. She would listen to the woman's story and commiserate because 'all men were idiots'. Rainy would gently lead the 'model' by the hand when they entered her studio. As the woman looked at the art, Rainy would softly whisper that she only painted the most beautiful women. She was fully engaged in making the woman as comfortable as possible. Rainy never rushed. Sometimes the session did start as a portrait. Most often it evolved into a nude pose. Repositioning an arm led to whisper kisses on the neck and a light caress of the lower back. They would kiss deeply and for a long time. Rainy sometimes stopped there so the woman would come back. It gave her something to look forward too. The women always came.

Chapter 13

Roger was Rainy's meal ticket. She would do anything to keep him interested. For months he was in a fog of lust. He had never met anyone like her and no one had ever manipulated him. She could make him do almost anything.

Rainy knew Roger had a stash of money hidden either on the Catch 'Em or in the cottage. At first she tried to convince herself she didn't care because he freely gave her any cash she wanted. The problem was she knew men. She knew he would tire of her no matter how she satisfied him. It was just what men do. She also knew Roger killed Freddy and that she could easily be his next victim. She began to look for his stash. She needed to have some escape money.

When Roger went drinking down at the Little Bar, Rainy searched the boat. When he went fishing, she searched the cottage. So far she had not found anything.

She continued to persuade women to come back to her studio. She did actually paint some portraits for a fee but mostly she seduced the 'models' and took them to bed. After endlessly teasing Roger, she needed the satisfaction she only got from loving willing women.

One afternoon she met a particularly sensual dark haired young Latina named Sofia who she found sitting alone in the coffee shop. Her man was fishing more and more and leaving her behind. She jumped at the chance to go home with Rainy. They barely got into the cottage before the cover ups and brief bikinis each wore were on the floor.

For weeks Rainy and Sofia got together every time their men went fishing. They often met at the Harbor Island Spa and enjoyed side by side massage. In the steam room their sweat slicked bodies merged in a special rhythm.

"Sofia, how long have you been with this man?" Rainy asked one afternoon when they had come back to the cottage.

"Not yet a year. What about you?"

"About the same. What will you do?"

"About what?"

"About when your man fuckin' dumps you?" Rainy sipped a bottle of water. "Don't pretend you haven't thought about it."

"Just come here and kiss me."

Rainy and Sofia lay in each others arms. Neither willing to talk about the future but each knowing it loomed like an island rage.

Chapter 14

Slowly Roger got more interested in fishing. He and his buddies would troll for marlin near Bimini and dock the Catch 'Em at the Anchorage Marina. He might be gone three or four days. Rainy didn't care at first. She knew he would come back. She figured he went on these fishing trips in part to make himself feel manly because when he did come back he was insatiable. She was happy to indulge his fantasies because when he was gone she could indulge hers.

Sofia told Rainy that her man was going to move his yacht to the Florida Keys soon. Now Rainy really began to think how vulnerable she was to Roger's whims. She had some very dark thoughts about how to get his money.

Rainy searched every inch of the cottage. She felt a sense of urgency because fishing was starting to be more important than fucking in their relationship. She could compete with other women, but this fishing obsession was undefeatable.

She knew he often left for the Little Bar by going through the workshop studio and down the back alley behind the cottage. She began searching along this route. She figured the stash had to be sizable because Roger didn't seem to have any other source of income. She also found it maddening that she could not find anything at all that identified who he really was.

Rainy knew how to manipulate men and women with her sensuality. She had done so with Roger but now sensed it was becoming less effective. She also knew he liked to be dominated and that he could possibly become a willing supplicant for more physical activities. She decided to transform her studio into a sex dungeon to try to keep him interested.

She added more erotic art, covered the windows and built a St. Andrews cross. She was moving her easel when one of the wooden support feet caught on a crack in the floor. At first Rainy was simply annoyed then realized she had never noticed this deviation in what otherwise was a smooth concrete slab. Using a pry bar she lifted a trap door that revealed the ten by ten room below.

Rainy knew immediately what she had found. She climbed down the ladder and even in the dim light could see stacks of money wrapped in clear plastic. She felt relief. Now she could plan for the inevitable day when Roger would dump her. She reasoned she could steal some of the cash. She just needed to make sure she wasn't caught. She had not forgotten about Captain Freddy and knew how rough Roger could be from their increasingly physical sex. He would kill her.

She decided to put the easel back where it was. She knew if she changed things too much he would get suspicious. Now her faux dungeon could just be staging for her painting. At least that was what she told him when he came home that evening.

"It all looks pretty kinky." He picked up a riding crop.

"Well these rich bitches love it."

"I might too." He slapped his thigh.

"Uh huh. You want to play?" Rainy dropped her cover up to reveal her completely hairless body. Roger responded as she knew he would and they spent the next few hours roleplaying in the dungeon.

54

She invited Sofia over a few days later after Roger had taken the Catch 'Em out for another fishing trip. She found the more time she spent with Roger the more desperate she became to feel a woman's touch. Sofia was a willing participant in restraint and teasing. After, they went for a swim in the clear water by the boat slip.

"I think I only have a few more days here." Sofia said over her shoulder as she climbed the ladder to the dock.

"Why do we do this to ourselves?" Rainy asked as she toweled off. "All I've ever done is bend my life around what men want."

Sofia sighed. "It's our life."

"Would you change if you could?"

"I don't think about it. I mean, what else can I do? " Sofia wrapped up in a towel and sat on the edge of the dock.

"Yeah, I know. It's all about money. These men have it and we don't. What if we could get some?"

"Now you talking crazy. Some? Need more than some. I ain't going back to working on the street."

"What would happen if you weren't around when your man is ready to move his boat?'

"Shit. that man would hunt me down. He can't get sweet pussy like mine even with all his money. Why you talking like this?"

"I'm just tired of living to keep some asshole happy. This guy, Roger is starting to think he can get a woman anytime 'cause of his good looks and charm. He's gonna dump me, and soon. Just want to get a jump on it."

"But what you gonna do? You got some cash put away?"

Rainy smiled. "Come with me." They crossed the street and went through the cottage to the studio.

"If I had money, would you be with me?" Rainy caressed Sofia's face. She responded by coming into her arms and they kissed for a long time.

"You just setting us up for sadness." Sofia sighed.

"Maybe not." Rainy started to move the easel and Sofia helped. Then Rainy opened the trapdoor. She grabbed a flashlight and climbed down into the dark room.

"What is this place." Sofia asked when she got to the bottom of the ladder.

"Well, not sure what it was built for but right now it is Roger's bank. Look at this." Rainy shined the light on the packages. "Pick up one of those packages."

"Damn! How much?"

"Don't know but plenty for us to get the fuck away."

"That man will kill you."

"Yeah, he will but he don't know I found his stash."

"What are you gonna do?"

"Not sure. You in?"

"If we can stay together." She leaned back in Rainy's arms.

"Well that's the plan. We just have to figure out a way to move it, then get off this fucking island.

"Where did all this come from?"

"Don't know, but I'm sure he stole it."

"Yeah. I mean why else would he keep it in this hole?"

"So if he finds out I know the mother fucker will kill

me and you too. It's that simple. I think if you help me we can get away."

"How?"

"Gonna kill him." Her face was hard and her eyes fixed.

Sofia looked at Rainy's expression and knew she was serious. Her path probably was just as rough to get where they were today. Both started out as 'trailer trash' but she had not killed anyone yet. Though the thought didn't shake her much.

"Yeah, then what?" Sofia started back up the ladder.

"Get the fuck off this island."

"How? You can't fly with a shit load of cash."

"I know. Don't have a passport either."

"How'd you get here?"

"I hid in the engine room of the boat Roger stole after he killed the owner." Rainy said.

"Damn, guy's a gangster. How you gonna kill the big mother?" Sofia wondered.

"Not sure yet but I think if I don't he's gonna kill me."

"Why?"

"He's getting more bizarre and wants me to peg him and shit. One of these times he's gonna just get pissed and beat me to death. He knows nobody would care. He could just throw my ass off his boat." Rainy's eyes were tearing up.

"Okay, this be crazy. Just come with me. I can talk my guy into taking you with us. Just tell him I'm recruiting you for a threesome and he'll do it."

"He hasn't even seen me. Why would he let me on his boat?"

"He's a Dominican man. Trust me. This man's always sniffing around American women. That's how I know he's getting tired of me. We can just keep him interested 'til we can get away from here," Sofia said.

"I don't know. If Roger's money's gone he'll go crazy and search all over. What if your boat, what's the name of it?"asked Rainy.

"El Conquistador"

"Of course it is. God damn boys and their toys. What if El Conquistador don't leave right away?"

"Rainy, settle down. We can figure this out."

"What about the passport thing?"

"We can buy one easy. I did. Just get a handful of cash."

"How are we going to get the rest of the money on your boat?"

"Look Rainy, we got to think this through. Give me some money and I'll get you a passport."

"Well, we need to figure it out quick."

"Yeah, come over later and meet Luis. He will drool all over you. He'll be back from fishing this afternoon."

"Bet he'll be all horny?"

Sofia laughed. "Yeah, he always is. Don't know what catching those stinking fish has to do with fucking but he comes home just ready to go."

"Must be something to do with handling those big trolling rods...Roger does the same thing. Can't wait to bend me over. At least he won't be back for a few days."

"Good. Dress sexy and meet me over at the Glass

Bridge Bar about seven. I'll act like you're an old friend from Key West. We'll soften ol' Luis up and get you out of here."

Rainy knew she was playing a dangerous game. If Roger got any idea she had found his money and was going to steal some or all of it she was sure he would brutally kill her. She gave Sofia $500 from her spending money to buy a passport.

She wanted to get an idea of how much there was in the 'money room' so she climbed back down with a flashlight and a pen and paper and measuring tape. She counted $10,000 in a bundle and there were about 1000 bundles. So, somewhere around 10 million dollars. When she measured 1 million she found it was a stack roughly 8 inches by 6 inches by 13 inches and weighed about 20 pounds. She took one $10,000 bundle for an emergency fund. She figured Roger would never miss it. She climbed back out and put things back so if Roger came home unexpectedly he wouldn't know she was on to his stash.

Rainy decided that she would put on a very sexy little black dress and see if she could manipulate Luis into taking her on his boat. Then she and Sofia could figure out how to steal the money. Maybe she wouldn't have to kill Roger.

Chapter 15

The Frostville Police Chief, Wilbur Bonnet retired after thirty one years in law enforcement. He had a few regrets. One was that he never caught Harvey Hall.

He was a lifelong bachelor and the townspeople of Frostville were his family. Many had been duped in the insurance scam as he had and some had been ruined in the collapse of the Oakmont development. That had been three years ago but, as he often said, the case was still open as long as he was alive.

At his retirement party he was given an all expense paid trip to pursue his passion of fishing. Wilbur had always thought that police work was a lot like trying to catch those wily critters.

About a week after he had cleaned out his desk he boarded a flight for Miami and a final destination of Islamorada for the fishing trip of a lifetime. He had only ever caught freshwater fish in the local farm ponds and was excited to have the opportunity to go after some serious game fish in the famous fishing grounds off of the Florida Keys.

Wilbur Bonnet was a short stout man. He smiled easily but more than thirty years in law enforcement had saturated him with a skeptical intuition and powerful observation skills. He quickly sized up the professional fishing community in and around Islamorada. He could tell that some of the charter captains were hustlers and some were hard working professionals. He chose one of these stalwarts to spend his first three days with.

Wilbur caught a few small fish but nothing like the monster marlin he dreamed about. He was bemoaning this fact to the bartender in the Lorelei Tiki Bar after another uneventful day of catching minnows. A fellow elbow bender sitting on the next stool nodded knowingly.

"Ya know, sometimes it's just dumb luck. Been working on these boats all my life, don't matter how much ya don't know if you drop your line on top of a big 'un. Look at ol' Captain Freddy. Couldn't find his ass with both hands and drags in the Florida record."

Wilbur looked at the man skeptically. "You mean this guy, what you say his name was?"

"Captain Freddy's all I ever knew him by."

"So this Captain Freddy is a number one fuck up and he's got the Florida record? For what kind of fish, a pompano?"

"Hell no man, Captain Freddy caught the record marlin. Over a thousand pounds, it was."

"Sorry my friend, just don't believe it. Takes too much skill to catch a fish like that."

"Damn, Jake this guy don't believe that Freddy caught the record." He said to the bartender.

"Hey don't get mad." Wilbur signalled for Jake to give the man a round on him.

"Ain't mad man. Jake, where's that picture at? The one that was in the paper. Thanks for the drink. Squiggy's the name by the way." They shook hands.

Jake reached up behind the cash register and removed a framed picture and put it on the bar in front of Wilbur. "Here you go. I wasn't working around here at the time but I've heard the story about a hundred times."

61

Wilbur looked at the huge fish hanging from the scales at the marina. The number 1061 was painted on the fish's body with white paint. Two tall guys flanked the dead fish. One with shaggy hair and a goofy smile and the other fully bearded with a hat pulled part way over his face.

"Now this is what I came down here to catch." Wilbur smiled and indicated to Jake for another round for his new friend Squiggy. "Is this Captain Freddy still around?"

"Naw, strangest kind of shit man, ol' Freddy was so happy after he caught that fish. He was the king. Don't make no sense that he would go somewheres else where nobody gives a shit but ain't seen him in a couple of years."

"So he just up and disappeared?", Chief Bonnet asked.

"Yep, 'bout two or three weeks after he caught the big one."

"He didn't tell anyone where he was going? I mean don't you guys kinda make sure somebody knows so if you have trouble with your boat someone would come looking?"

"Yeah, that's how it works. Just ol' Freddy he didn't fish regular like. Kinda did his own thing. Still strange cause like I said he was so proud of that fish."

"What do you mean he did his own thing?" Wilbur took a sip of his drink.

"Well all the charter guys 'cept Freddy are booked through the marina. Everyone takes turns unless a customer requests your boat. Freddy kinda just had one guy that came down from somewhere about every two or three weeks and they would go off fishing. He's the other guy in the picture." Squiggy stabbed at the picture with his finger.

"Know his name?" Wilbur was curious now.

"Naw, never knew." Squiggy downed his drink and slid off the stool. "Gotta get home, early morning going to Bimini. You gonna fish?"

"Yeah on the Dawn Lee."

Squiggy laughed. "My boat. So see ya in the morning."

Chapter 16

Rainy and Sofia underestimated their men. Roger and Luis knew each other. They were part of a very close-knit fishing fraternity. Men with money and a desire to catch record marlin all traveled in the same circle. They collaborated on equipment and shared some information. Of course they also were extremely competitive so they never gave away their top fish catching secrets.

In the bar of the Anchorage Marina on Bimini many tales were told. The stories started out being about fishing but after endless rounds of rum or whiskey the men bragged about their money. Inevitably though the topic turned to women. These were men who 'kept' women. Their yachts were magnets for young beautiful girls that were always hanging around the docks. The men indulged and frequently swapped or traded them like fishing tips. Of course wives and children were left at home.

Roger was new to the scene but caught on quickly. He had thought he was just lucky to have Rainy waiting for him back in Spanish Wells, but learned that she was as expendable as yesterday's bait.

The men boasted about the various talents their women had. Roger shared stories about Rainy's dominatrix tendencies and one guy in particular was more than interested. His name was Luis Abelard from the Dominican Republic. He had a 75 foot fishing machine named El Conquistador. Soon they had descended into some kind of alcohol-driven macho deal making.

"I got me this little doe eyed Dominican girl. She a good fuck." Luis ordered a couple of more shots.

Roger was so drunk he was having trouble leaning against the bar. He knocked back another shot though. "You want exciting? You want exciting? I got this crazy bitch with her face tattooed on her shoulder. She will light you up like that marlin you lost today."

Luis put his arm around Roger's shoulders. "We get back, we trade. I need some new stuff." The men clinked shot glasses.

"When you going back?" Luis was very interested,

"Couple of days." Roger knew he had to get back to the Catch 'Em before he passed out.

"Don't forget our deal."

Roger nodded as he wobbled out of the bar.

The next day Luis was nursing a huge hangover and decided not to fish. He had his crew take El Conquistador back to Harbor Island while he slept.

When the boat docked he stumbled over to the condo he rented to find Sofia. She was looking particularly good and helped him forget how bad he felt. She was so sweet he almost changed his mind about 'trading' her to Roger.

"Do you want to go out for a drink?" Sofia smiled.

"We can. Think I can handle one now." Luis kind of grimaced.

"Poor baby." Sofia caressed his face. "Just one. I need to get out."

They took the short walk down to the Glass Bridge Bar and as regulars were welcomed by the owner. He sat them at a corner booth and took their drink orders.

Spanish Wells was a ten minute ferry ride from Harbor Island and Rainy came over frequently in the morning for coffee and to pick up 'models'. She rarely visited in the evening.

Sofia saw Luis' eyes light up. *He is such a pig.* She knew why without even turning around. Rainy walked up to the bar in a little black dress and stilettos. She was wearing a long blond wig and gold choker necklace. The dress was cut so that the tattoo of her profile peeked out. When she sat at the bar men on either side immediately sent her drinks.

"I know that woman." Sofia had turned to look. "She lived in Key West when I did." She got up and went over to Rainy where they had a pretty convincing reunion.

Luis stood, bowed and kissed Rainy's hand with his best Dominican manners when Sofia brought her to their table. He made sure she was seated comfortably in the booth while ignoring Sofia. Normally this behavior would have ignited her Latin temper. She just sat quietly while Luis fawned over Rainy.

"Girl, what are you doing out here?" Sofia asked.

"Came over with a group of friends," she lied. "Just wanted to see a different island. Ya know?" She smiled at Luis.

"Yeah, I understand. All these sand bars start looking alike after a while. When you going back?"

"Not sure."

"I'm going to move my boat over to Islamorada. Would you like to ride along?" Luis was so polite and formal Sofia thought she would throw up.

"Great idea Luis. What do you think Rainy?"

"Might be fun." She placed her hand on Luis' thigh and leaned across him to kiss Sofia deeply.

"Let me show you my boat." Luis spouted a worn line directly out of a bad movie. He already had a raging hard on.

The girls laughed. They all moved out of the bar. "This is my little boat, El Conquistador." Luis pointed to 75 foot floating palace.

Of course Luis let Rainy go up the gangway in front of him so he could check out her ass as she climbed. It was only then that he saw her tattoo. Some vague memory started to form. He knew he should know something about a girl with her face tattooed on her shoulder but he just couldn't remember why.

Sofia turned on some pulsating island music and broke out the rum. Luis sat and watched as Rainy and Sofia danced. They ignored him and moved to their own rhythm. He got up to join them.

"Sit your ass down, you mother fucker." Rainy slapped him hard across the face. Luis stumbled back onto the couch. She moved over him.

"I'll tell you when to get up you puny worm." She smiled and danced back to Sofia. They kissed deeply. Rainy slithered back over to Luis and caressed him. He started to get up and she slapped him again.

"I can see you like it rough." Rainy danced away again. "Sofia, you fuck him. I've got to go." She left the boat.

The control and tease tactic worked. Luis begged Sofia to get Rainy to come with them to Florida.

"I don't know if she will come Luis but I'll go see her tomorrow and ask."

67

Chapter 17

In the morning Roger was still drunk when the Catch 'Em left the Anchorage Marina on Bimini. He mumbled something about catching a big one to his mate, Gregario then he disappeared into his cabin.

The wind and conditions were not good for trolling. Gregario put out the lines anyway. He and Higgs had decided to try it for a couple of hours at least until Roger sobered up.

"I mean the man pays us to fish, so's we might as well. What ya think?" Gregario had climbed up to the flybridge.

Higgs just nodded. "We might get lucky, we might."

Later, Roger woke up in a paranoid panic. He had been having a disjointed nightmare about running out of money. He looked around his cabin, the *owner's cabin* and calmed down. He knew he had plenty of cash as long as no one else knew where it was.

Lately though he had a creeping concern that Rainy might betray him. She did know he had killed Freddy and she obviously knew he had money hidden somewhere. She had not given him any reason not to trust her but now that he better understood this big game fishing culture he knew that women like Rainy were disposable. He lay there thinking that it was time to get rid of her and that's when he remembered his 'deal' with the guy that owned the El Conquistador. Luis was his name, he thought.

"Looks a bit sloppy." Roger had climbed up to the flybridge where Higgs was on the wheel and Gregario was watching the baits.

"Yeah it is, but never know." Higgs bumped the throttles to get on top of a wave. "Left engine's running rough."

"Yeah? I want to head back."

"Bimini?"

"No, back to Spanish Wells."

"No problem." Gregario nodded and slipped down to the cockpit and brought in the lines. Higgs put the Catch 'Em up on plane.

"Should be home in a couple of hours."

"Good. Going below."

Chapter 18

Sofia took the ferry over to Spanish Wells and hiked up to Roger's cottage to find Rainy. When no one came to the door she found it unlocked and made her way to the studio out back. She paused at the door when she heard noise. She was about to leave when Rainy appeared.

"I saw you come down off the porch," she whispered. "Roger's here."

Sofia nodded. "Yeah, we need to talk. Meet me at the coffee shop."

Sofia was about to finish her second cup when Rainy rushed in a bit tousled. "Sorry about that." She slid in the booth.

"When did he get home?"

"Last night. About two days early. Not sure why, mumbled something about engine trouble."

"Still horny I bet."

"Yeah. He's kind of tied up right now." She rolled her eyes.

"These men really like being treated like shit don't they?"

"Some sure do. He'll be perfectly content until I go back and untie him. Think it's some kind of 'mommy' thing."

"Must be. Luis is all hot to have you on our boat. I never treated him like you did. Guess I should have."

"It's not that easy. Took me a while to know how to punish 'em and not hurt 'em too bad. Seems like these rich guys like it though. Look, I gotta go back. Since I didn't expect Roger, I guess we'll have to figure out something else."

"Yeah, but hurry. Luis wants to go back to Florida as soon as the fishing season's over. Here's the passport I bought for you." She slid it across the table.

"Ok, I'll come over in the morning and we can meet up."

"Yeah, I'll try. Not having cell phone service is a pain. If I'm not there it's because Luis is all horny. If you can wait I'll come as soon as I can."

"Okay."

When Sofia didn't show up the next day, Rainy bought some wine and cheese as a reason for her trip. Then she took the ferry back to Spanish Wells. She found Roger and Higgs on the Catch'Em.

"Hi guys, what's going on?" Rainy climbed down into the engine room.

"Got some sorta problem. Think gonna have to pull the boat and replace the fucking engines."

Rainy could tell Roger was in a foul mood. He slipped into some kind of redneck speak when the boat was messed up. She knew to stay out of the way. So she just nodded and climbed back up the ladder. She looked over her shoulder and noticed that, while Higgs was checking out her bikini covered butt, Roger didn't even look her way. She knew he would get rid of her soon because a few months before he would have dropped what he was doing when she entered a room just to look at her.

Rainy sat in the salon to think. She could hear Roger and Higgs discussing what to do with the boat.

"Fucking spent a shit load for this tub and the god damn engines need to be replaced." Roger ranted.

"Might could rebuild 'em, you might." Higgs offered.

"Yeah, either way gonna miss the rest of the season."

"Could maybe fish with somebody?" Higgs was trying to be helpful.

"Yeah, guess." Roger pouted like a spoiled little boy. "Don't know who though."

"How 'bout that El Conquistador? He could use the help, he could. From what I know he don't catch much."

"Luis something. That was his name. Yeah, pretty good guy. Good idea Higgs." Roger brightened. "Me and him had a deal going anyway."

Rainy wanted to hear more but could tell Roger was about to come up from below. She went into the galley so he wouldn't think she was eavesdropping. She had heard enough to know that Roger and Luis knew each other. This was puzzling. She also heard Roger might want to fish with Luis on El Conquistador. Maybe knowing this might help her get away. Maybe, but it might make things more complicated. She needed to talk to Sofia.

"Rainy, I'm going over to Harbor Island. Don't wanna come, do ya?" Roger was less than enthusiastic in his request.

"Was over there this morning. Brought back some stuff for dinner. So I'll pass."

"Yeah, okay." Roger climbed over to the dock and walked toward the ferry.

Rainy could hear Higgs still banging away in the engine room. She decided to turn on the charm and pump him for some more information. She eased down the ladder and saw that he noticed her right away.

"What's wrong? Roger's all pissed." She asked.

"Well, not sure, not. But might gonna have to pull Catch'Em to find out."

"How long will that take?"

"The yard's really backed up. Roger can throw his money around. Still gonna take a couple weeks, it will." Higgs wiped his hands on a grease rag.

"Well shit like this happens all the time with boats, don't it?"

"Yeah, he knows that. He just don't want to miss out on the fishing?"

Rainy rolled her eyes. "So what's he gonna do?"

"Well think he's gonna hitch a ride on another boat, he is."

"Yeah? How's he do that?"

"All these fishermen know each other. Drink every night and talk shit. He knows this guy what got a big boat that would probably take him."

"What guy is that?"

"Some prick what owns a boat called El Conquistador."

This was the first time Rainy had ever heard Higgs not be totally solicitous of these rich guys. "Boys and their toys." She mumbled.

"Yeah, you got money you can play in their game." Higgs shut the tool box with a little more force than necessary.

"How do you stand being around these spoiled rich boys?" Rainy decided to take a chance and see if Higgs might be a possible accomplice.

"Not any other work out here."

"I get that. Don't you get sick of it?" Rainy leaned against the ladder.

"Yeah, Roger can throw me off his boat just 'cause we didn't catch a fish one day, he could,"

"I guess you get fucked just like me."

Higgs looked hard at Rainy. He understood they were really in same fix. She had never been friendly but she wasn't mean. "Look, I just try to make Roger happy same as you."

"I know. It just sucks. He's getting ready to dump me."

"Happens." Higgs pushed the tool box under a shelf. "Gotta go to the boat yard."

Rainy turned and climbed up the ladder with Higgs right behind. She knew he was getting a show. In the salon she turned to him. "If he dumps me can you help me get back to Florida?"

"Ain't no problem. Just get on a plane."

"What if I need to kinda sneak in?"

"Yeah, I see. No papers, huh?"

Rainy just shrugged not wanting to say more.

"Easy to do. Just need a little cash. Fishing boats going that way all the time."

"So you'll help?"

Higgs just nodded then climbed over to the dock and walked away. Rainy sat in the fighting chair to think. Things might change any minute but maybe if Roger goes out on the El Conquistador and Higgs doesn't she could pay him to get her back to Florida with a load of Roger's cash.

Chapter 19

Roger came back from Harbor Island about four in the morning and was very drunk. He shoved a naked Rainy out of bed, punched her in the gut and drug her to the 'Dungeon'.

Rainy slipped away from him.

"Heard you was fucking around over there." He nodded his head toward Harbor Island. "You only fuck around with me." He slurred and grabbed her wrist.

"What the fuck are you talking about?"

"Why were you on that boat?" He squeezed harder then slapped and backhanded her across the face.

He probably expected her to crumble but Rainy kicked him in the balls. She landed a direct blow and Roger went to his knees. She ran out of the studio and down the alley. She knew if she couldn't get away she was dead.

Since there is very little ambient light in Spanish Wells she was able to hide in the darkness under a stone overhang in the alley wall. Roger banged around in the studio and then staggered out of the door. He went by her still cussing and muttering. He soon was out of sight. Rainy just hunkered down. She hoped he would just pass out somewhere. She didn't care how he knew she had been on El Conquistador. She knew he was going to kill her. She was naked and trembling. If she didn't do something quick she had no chance to survive.

Rainy crept back into the studio. Roger had destroyed it. She had no idea when he would come back so she went into the cottage and threw on some clothes and put some in a bag. She grabbed the bundle of cash she had stolen for an emergency and fled out the front door. She ran down the road toward the ferry landing. She knew the first run to Harbor Island was right at sunrise. She hid between two parked trucks straining to hear any noise that might be Roger looking for her.

At daylight she heard voices which scared her at first but gave her a little comfort when she realized several people were loading onto the ferry. She slipped out of her hiding place and stepped off the seawall onto the small boat. The other passengers were maids and cooks that were heading to their jobs in the fancy hotels, cottages and restaurants on Harbor Island. They surreptitiously stared at her battered face but mostly ignored her.

Rainy moved into the small cabin so Roger would not be able to easily spot her from shore. Of course she had no idea where he was. Her first thought was to go to the El Conquistador and get help from Sofia but for all she knew Roger was on board with his new buddy, Luis.

After the short ride, Rainy decided to stay out of sight until she could figure out her next move. In the dim early morning light she walked to a nearby beach that had a covered picnic table. This gave her a vantage point to see if Roger came on shore. She had to think.

Chapter 20

Roger woke up outside the Little Bar. He was laying in the sand next to the trash cans. He had a massive hangover. He was dirty, disheveled and had lost one of his topsiders. People were walking about and the sun was pretty hot so he knew he had been out for a long time. On shaky legs he looked around for his shoe. When he couldn't find it he pulled the one off his foot and dropped it on the ground. Barefoot, he limped back to the cottage.

He sat for a minute on the porch steps. Everything was quiet and Catch 'Em rode easily in the slip across the street. The roaring in his head felt oddly incongruent with this peaceful scene. Flashes of the night before jolted into his consciousness. He knew he had been on El Conquistador with Luis. They agreed to fish together. In celebration they drank shots, many shots. He had danced with a dark haired girl while Luis made jokes about trading her to him.

Some how in the blur of the night Roger learned that Rainy had been on the boat. He paid one of Luis' crew to bring him back to Spanish Wells in a skiff because the ferry stopped running at midnight.

He remembered getting kicked in the balls by Rainy but not much after that. Now he thought he had better check on his money. That was all he really cared about.

When he walked through the cottage it was a mess. This was unusual. He crossed the back porch and entered the workshop/studio and opened the trapdoor. He slid down the ladder and glanced around through bloodshot eyes. It seemed that his money was safe.

He climbed out of the storage room and closed it up. He saw that the studio had been destroyed and now remembered his rage.

Up in the cottage bedroom drawers were pulled open and clothes scattered about. Rainy was gone but his money was safe. He crawled under the covers and went to sleep.

Rainy decided to check into the Harbor Island Hotel. The pompous clerk looked a bit disdainful. Rainy's hair was matted and greasy. She had on booty shorts, a tank top, no bra and flip flops. Her eyes were swollen and bruised. There was a red welt on the side of her face. She didn't look like the type of clientele the hotel generally catered to. When Rainy brought out a wad of hundreds his haughty attitude disappeared. She was quickly checked in.

Rainy lay on the bed with ice from the hallway machine on her face. She thought her cheek bone might be broken. She would just have to deal with it herself.

She was trying to guess what Roger might do next. She suspected that he would again fly into a rage and try to hunt her down. She also reasoned that if she could get back to the States he probably would not follow. After all she knew he killed Freddy and she was sure the money was stolen. She had enough cash to buy her way onto a fishing boat, or with the fake passport, she could fly home. It wasn't enough. She wanted to take all of it from that son of a bitch. She never wanted to be some guy's property again. She needed to talk to Sofia.

Roger woke up late in the afternoon. He made it into the shower and got into some clean clothes. He walked to the coffee shop. He slid into a booth where Higgs was eating a grilled cheese sandwich.

"Not lookin too good there captain. Carla, bring this man some coffee." Higgs was back to being solicitous. He had no interest in getting involved with Rainy's drama because Roger was his meal ticket.

Roger's hand shook when he raised the coffee mug. "Tough night." Higgs just nodded. "You seen Rainy?"

Higgs shook his head without comment.

"Had some drinks with that El Conquistador guy. Gonna fish with him for the last week of the season."

Higgs looked up. "Am I going with you?" He needed the work.

"Naw, but do got a job for you." Higgs just looked at him. "Find Rainy and keep her from leaving."

"Not exactly what I do there captain, it ain't." Higgs took a sip from his mug.

"I'll pay your daily rate."

"What am I supposed to do when I find her?"

"Keep her from leaving the island."

"Sounds like kidnapping to me, it does."

"Double your day rate plus a thousand when I get back." Roger was getting impatient. "Can't be too hard to find her. You know everybody and she ain't got no papers."

"What do I do with her?"

"Put her in the cottage and keep her there. Tie her up, I don't care." Roger was getting angry.

"Gonna cost you more'n a double rate."

"Yeah, just find her. Use the radio on the Catch 'Em and call me on El Conquistador later." Roger took one last sip of coffee and left.

"Carla, you got any of that pie left?" Higgs asked. He ate it as he thought about Roger's request. So Rainy must have dumped Roger before he could dump her and now he wanted her back. Typical of these spoiled rich guys. Always want what they can't have. He was sure he could find her if she was still around. He just needed to put out the word. He wasn't sure about keeping her in the cottage. That really crossed the line. He could be pretty shady but he didn't want to take a kidnapping fall for Roger's sorry ass while he went fishing with his new best buddy on El fuckin' Conquistador.

Chapter 21

On the small porch of the third floor room in the Harbor Island Hotel, Rainy could see El Conquistador in the marina. She watched the service people and crew coming and going. Judging by the activity she thought the boat was being readied for a trip. She knew the season had about a week left so it made sense that Roger would be on board at some point. She watched a gas truck pull up and begin the long process of refueling the large yacht.

Sofia appeared at the top of the gangway. She started down then stopped as if she had been called to and climbed back up where Luis was standing on the deck. Of course Rainy could not hear the conversation but their gestures looked like they were quarreling. Sofia turned and headed back down to the dock. She walked determinedly down the quay.

Rainy quickly left her room and ran down the stairwell. She crossed the lobby just as Sofia walked past.

"Sofia." Rainy called to her as she exited the automatic doors.

"Rainy! Oh my god, what happened?" Sofia hugged her then pulled back to look at her face.

"Quick, come with me." Rainy turned back into the lobby with Sofia right behind.

In the room, Rainy went out to the porch to see if Roger was anywhere to be seen.

"Rainy, what are you doing?" Sofia moved to the porch rail.

"Just want to see if Roger's near. The son of a bitch tried to kill me last night." She moved back into the room.

"Yeah, he and Luis were fuckin' wasted. I thought Roger was still on board."

"The big mother fucker dragged my ass out of bed about four this morning. If he hadn't been so drunk I probably would be dead. How did he know I had been on El Conquistador?"

"He and Luis were laughing and joking about trading me for you. Somehow they figured out that you had come on board. It all had to do with your tattoo. Roger got really pissed. Luis egged him on. Told him to fuck me so they could seal their trade. Roger got really physical and tried but he couldn't get it up."

"Yeah when he drinks he gets like that."

"Then I locked myself in a guest cabin. Didn't hear anything more. A little while ago me and Luis got in to it and I left."

"Well somehow he got back to the cottage," Rainy said. "He beat me but I managed to kick him in the balls and get away. Not sure where he went then but I got some of my stuff and hid out 'til I could get the ferry over here. I checked in about two hours ago."

"Shit." Sofia sat on the bed. She softly caressed Rainy's face. "That bastard."

"Yeah, but I got an idea. Are those idiots going fishing?"

"You know they are. Nothing gets in the way of chasing those fuckin' fish. Heard Luis tell his captain to be ready to leave this afternoon. He wants to have lines in the water at daybreak tomorrow."

"So I have to stay hidden."

"Yeah and I have to wait in the condo for Luis to come crawling over all sorry and shit. He's such a pussy. Makes me want to puke. You know Roger is gonna look for you."

"Yeah, I figure he might not expect me to be here. But I'm only buying a little time. If I can hide out till he and Luis leave, maybe we can get off this fucking island."

"Does he know you found his stash?"

"Nope. If he did he would have killed me while I was asleep. I took only one bundle so I can't see how he would miss it."

"You know he'll hire an island creep to look for you. These locals will give you up in a heartbeat."

"I know, one reason I'm not going to the clinic." She gently touched her cheek. "Just figure if they go off fishing before he discovers where I am, we might have a chance."

"So I'll go to the condo and wait for Luis to come apologize", Sofia said. "When the boat leaves I'll come find you and we'll figure some way out of here."

Rainy nodded and the two women hugged for a long time. They both knew it was a risky plan.

Chapter 22

Roger gathered the clothes, the stolen passport and gear he needed to fish with Luis. He loaded it into the golf cart and drove over to the ferry landing. There he hired a water taxi instead of waiting for the scheduled ferry. The small boat took him right to the dock beside El Conquistador. Luis sent some of his crew to help get everything on board.

"Brought my favorite rod and some gear. Okay with you?" Luis just nodded. Roger was back to being charming. He didn't like having to fish on someone else's boat but he didn't have much of a choice since the Catch 'Em was out of commission.

Luis was happy to have a knowledgeable angler who could catch a marlin on board. He had not been able to do it by himself. Plus he was eager to have a chance with that crazy Rainy.

"That tattoo girl coming?"

"She took off." Luis looked disappointed.

"Man, thought that was our deal."

"Yeah, got somebody looking for her. Maybe find her before we leave. If not she'll be here when we get back. Don't want no women around while we fish."

"You're right they always whine and fuck things up." Luis brightened, "we can trade when we get back." Luis showed Roger the cabin he would use.

"We'll shove off soon as fueling is done. I gotta go see Sofia, so make yourself at home."

"Hey, tell her next time she'll get a full dose of ol' Roger."

Luis left the boat and walked over to the condo. He found Sofia lounging by the pool in the back. She was totally nude.

"Looking good, chica." He smiled.

"Don't bring me that shit. You trying to pimp me to that big white mother fucker."

"Ah baby, just having a little fun. How bout a taste before I go?" Luis moved between her legs. She was about to shut him down but decided to keep him happy because she always did. Maybe this time might be the last.

Rainy had seen Roger go on board the El Conquistador from the porch of her room. She then saw Luis walk to the condo. These men are so predictable she thought. Now if she could stay hidden until they go off fishing maybe she and Sofia would have a chance to get away.

Chapter 23

Higgs told the ferry boat captain, who was his cousin, that he was looking for Rainy and would pay for information. The island telegraph did the rest. All he had to do was sit in the coffee shop and wait. Within two hours the morning shift of maids was back in Spanish Wells. Two of them stopped by and told Higgs they had seen Rainy on the ferry and later in the Harbor Island Hotel. A bellman, another cousin, gave him the room number. The information cost Higgs about a hundred dollars.

Instead of letting Roger know, he would call the El Conquistador later and say he was still looking. He didn't want to make it seem so easy. In the mean time he could keep an eye on Rainy through his contacts. He hadn't decided whether or not he wanted to try to hold her in the cottage. He thought that was pretty extreme for a lover's spat even for a rich asshole like Roger.

Luis believed he had smoothed things over with Sofia when he left the condo because they had sex. He thought he was some great lover and she was so happy to be with him. In reality Sofia just tolerated his limp attempts at lovemaking because it was the way she stayed off the street. She knew, like Rainy did, that her day to day life was tentative and controlled by a man. She was always relieved when he went off fishing. It gave her a break. The big problem this time was this idea of being traded to Roger for Rainy. This was pretty slimy even for Luis who she knew had no feelings. She decided to clean up and go find Rainy. Maybe they could get away from both of these assholes.

Luis climbed up the gangway. He gave a thumbs up to the captain. He heard the engines rumbled to life.

"Looks like some nice weather." Roger appeared. He handed Luis a Red Stripe. They clinked bottles.

"Gotta good feeling about this trip."

Rainy saw the big yacht start down the channel. She felt some sense of relief but was still wary. She knew Roger thought of her as a possession and he was not going to easily give her up.

Higgs learned Rainy had checked into the Harbor Island Hotel under a different name and that she paid cash. Not surprising he thought. Somewhere else she might have remained anonymous but on this small island there was really nowhere to hide. Of course he would not let Roger know that. As far as he was concerned Higgs was conducting an all out search. That's how he described it when he called the El Conquistador on the marine radio. Roger just reiterated that he was to find Rainy at any cost and to hold her until he returned. He was to call again the next day, or sooner, if he had news.

Higgs let a full day go by before he called Roger. He got an ear full of posturing. He also heard Roger say he would up the 'bounty' to $20,000. This got a promise from Higgs that he was closing in and would have Rainy when Roger returned.

Up until this point Higgs had just kept tabs on Rainy through his contacts. He knew she was still checked in the hotel. He knew she was spending time with the woman on the El Conquistador. This made him suspicious and wary. Was he getting into the middle of some weird sex thing? He didn't like it but $20,000 was more than he made most years. He decided to capture Rainy and take her to the cottage.

He met with a couple of his Little Bar buddies to get their help. Over beers he laid out what he needed to do. These guys were fishermen like Higgs but all of them had done shady drug deals to survive. A few times things had gotten ugly and dangerous so kidnapping one woman seemed easy.

Higgs had the key to Rainy's room. One of his gang had a skiff and they made their way over to the dock behind the Harbor Island Hotel. The bellman opened the back emergency exit and all of them went up the staircase.

It was after three AM and no one was in the corridor. Higgs carefully unlocked the door. He knew there would be a security chain. One of the guys had a small bolt cutter but the door swung open. They crept in. Higgs turned on the light. The bed was empty. He saw that there were some clothes and personal items about so he figured she was just out. He turned off the light and told his guys to get comfortable. They would wait.

At daybreak the would be kidnappers snuck out of the hotel. Higgs felt some urgency. He had been pretty confident that he knew where Rainy was. Now he wasn't too sure. He wanted to check with his contacts at the airport to see if she had boarded a flight. So they took the skiff to the north end of Eleuthera. The ticket agent said that no woman meeting Rainy's description had flown out in the last day or so. Higgs headed back to Spanish Wells. He would put out the word and promise more cash for information.

Chapter 24

Rainy woke up in Sofia's arms. It was her first decent night's sleep since being dragged out of bed and beaten by Roger. Her face still hurt but the swelling had gone down.

"You look a little better this morning." Sofia was smiling. "Glad you came over last night."

"Yeah, finally got some sleep. Been waiting for someone to kick down that hotel room door." Rainy slid to the edge of the bed.

"Think you should just stay here. Don't even go back to the hotel. You know Roger's got spies and he will find you." Sofia got out of bed and put on a bikini.

"What happens when those two idiots get back from fishing?"

"We can go to the airport and fly to Miami. I've got my passport and the one I bought for you will work."

"I know that's the easiest thing to do but I'm not leaving without the cash." Rainy dressed in a t shirt, shorts and flip flops. "I'm going over to Spanish Wells and hire a boat, shit I'll buy one if I have to."

"You can't run it by yourself." Sofia said.

"Don't plan to. There are enough out of work fishermen that I can hire a crew."

"How do you keep them from throwing your ass overboard?"

"Well, you have to come to watch my back."

"You know I'll come but the two of us aren't much match for a crew."

"Well I knew that Freddy had a gun. I found it on his boat and hid it on the Catch 'Em."

"If we are going to do this let's not wait around. Never know when El Conquistador will come back." Sofia took a small overnight bag from her closet and packed some clothes.

"Don't take much. Let Luis think you are still here. It might buy us some time. I'm not going back to the hotel. Roger probably knows I'm checked in by now. Just let his spies think I'm still there."

Just as Rainy and Sofia stepped off the ferry in Spanish Wells, Higgs was coming up the channel in his buddy's skiff. He spotted Rainy right away.

"I'll be damned, there she is. Put in at the seawall."

Higgs stepped out of the skiff. He followed Rainy and a woman he figured was off the El Conquistador. He realized that he could simply be friendly because Rainy should not have any reason to fear him. When he got closer he could see that she had a bruised face. Now he wondered how crazy Roger might be. The money he would get for kidnapping her started to seem like a poor reason to get tangled up in some abusive bullshit.

"Hey there Rainy, know where Roger is?"

She was startled but quickly decided that Higgs was not a threat. "Went off fishing on El Conquistador. He didn't tell you?"

"Naw, last I saw him he was just talking about it, he was." Higgs played dumb.

"Left a few days ago with her guy." She nodded toward Sofia.

"Figured he did something like that. He wanted me to work on his boat which I done. Turns out it was no big repair. Just gotta finish up."

"Don't know nothing about that." Rainy continued to walk toward the cottage. It wasn't like Higgs was asking permission. She was thinking about enlisting him to help her get off the island since she had broached the subject a few days earlier.

In front of the cottage Higgs headed over to the boat slip. Rainy looked at Sofia. "Look, I'm gonna talk to him. Wait for me in the cottage."

Rainy stepped onto the Catch 'Em. She found Higgs looking down into the engine room. "Hey, can I talk to you?" Higgs nodded and moved out to the salon where Rainy sat down on the couch.

"Higgs, I think you and me are kinda in the same fix." She self consciously touched her face.

"Naw missy, ain't nobody smacked me in the face. Leastwise not some pussy like Roger. He beat you?"

She nodded. "Not what I meant. I have to keep that asshole happy and so do you."

He nodded. "True, that is." He was really struggling. He knew she had no idea Roger wanted her kidnapped. He was thinking that if she was just some rich air head it would be easy but he knew she was right about them being in a similar fix.

"Look missy you need to get the fuck off this island."

Rainy nodded. "I know."

"No you don't. That fucker wants me to kidnap you and tie you up til he gets back."

"What?" Rainy felt ill.

"Yeah, said he would pay me big bucks to do it."

"So you've changed your mind?"

"Not worth it. You ain't done nothin, you ain't."

"Does he know I'm still around?"

"Yeah, I call him on the El fuckin' Conquistador every day from this boat. Was gonna tell him today that I had you." Rainy looked puzzled. "I knew which room you was in, had the key and everything. Was gonna drag your ass back here."

"But I was gone."

Higgs nodded. "Saw you getting off the ferry though so you made it easy."

"So you lied about not knowing he went fishing on El Conquistador?" Higgs nodded. "But now you don't want Roger's money?"

"Not worth it. He's a prick. I remember what you said about him dumping you and I figure you dumped him first."

"Look Higgs I think I know a way to stick it to him and still get you paid. You in?"

"Don't know, you should just get the hell out of here."

"I am but first I got an idea. What do you think?"

"Ain't sure but I'm listening."

"You said the Catch 'Em is fixed?"

"Yeah, pretty much."

"How 'bout you radio Roger and tell him you got me tied up in the cottage." Rainy got off the couch and started pacing around the salon.

"Easy enough, then what?"

"We take the Catch 'Em to Florida and sell her."

"You crazier than me. How you gonna sell his boat?"

"The paperwork's sketchy. His name ain't on it. Just some LLC. I know I can bullshit some buyer into it if the price is right. I saw Roger do it with the boat we came here in."

"I don't know. Sounds pretty risky," Higgs shook his head.

"Okay, how much was he gonna pay you to kidnap me?"

"Maybe as much as twenty grand."

"How much you think Catch 'Em is worth?"

"Worth about a quarter mil, I'd say."

"So we sell her for 200 thousand and you get half."

Higgs scratched his head. "He'll report her stolen, chase us."

"Might but if we get into US water he won't follow."

"How do you know?"

"'Cause he killed the owner of the boat we came over here on. Roger ain't going near US water." Of course Rainy wasn't saying anything about the hidden money. She liked the plan she had concocted. If Higgs would do it she and Sofia could secretly load the boat with the cash.

"What? Roger killed a boat owner? Who?"

"Guy named Freddy Brovania de Maurice. I used to live with him in Islamorada."

"Did he have a boat named The Baron?" Higgs asked.

Rainy was confused. "He did, that's the boat Roger stole and sold."

"Small world ain't it? That guy killed my brother."

"Freddy killed your brother?" Rainy looked astounded. "I knew Freddy for a long time, he was a little nuts but never knew him to be violent."

"Crazy connection between his Grandfather and my family, it was. Goes way back to 1940's."

"I don't know what that all means but The Baron was the boat and Roger killed Freddy. Its one reason I know he won't go back to the States."

"Yeah, and a reason to kill you. You just need to get the hell out of here."

"I am, but we need your help. I mean look let's just go. We can be in Florida before Roger even knows his boat's gone. Get on the radio and tell him you got me. That way he won't be in a hurry to get back."

"You said we. Who is we?"

"Me and Sofia. She is going too."

"So we gonna have that El Conquistador prick chasing us too?"

"Probably but maybe not. Sofia says Luis, the owner is a pussy. She says he will just buy another girl."

"She got a passport?"

"Yeah it got her here, so kinda legit. Mine, not so much."

"You got enough money for fuel and dock fees?", Rainy nodded.

"This is crazy but I'll do it. Be ready to go in an hour." Higgs looked at Rainy then stepped over to the dock and walked away.

Rainy found Sofia in the kitchen making coffee. "Hey, we got less than an hour to move as much cash as we can to Catch 'Em." Rainy headed toward the studio.

Sofia caught up inside and helped open the trapdoor. "So this guy is going to help us?" Rainy nodded. "Did you tell him about the cash?"

"Nope. I'll explain what's in it for him later. Right now we need to move this money."

With a wheelbarrow and motivation, it didn't take long for Rainy and Sofia to empty the storage room and hide the money on the Catch 'Em.

When Higgs returned, Rainy was handing a box full of supplies from the dock to Sofia.

"Got everything you need?" Higgs jumped down into the boat. He had only one small sea bag.

"We do. Bottled water, food, beer. "

"Stand by the bow and stern lines and let me get her running." Higgs climbed to the flybridge.

A few minutes later Higgs nodded to the girls. They untied the lines. He backed the Catch 'Em out of the slip and turned down the channel. Rainy and Sofia went into the galley to put the food away.

"I just grabbed anything I could find and emptied the fridge. We have plenty to get us at least to a marina in Florida."

"I have to tell you I'm still scared. Luis and Roger together are freaky. They will chase us." Sofia's hand shook as she picked up a can of beans.

Rainy hugged her. "I know but look we've got a good head start. Its a big ocean. We just need to get as far from here as we can."

"But won't Roger know you went back to Florida?"

"Yeah, but I don't think he'll come after me. Besides, what's he gonna use for money?"

"That's the thing, he's gonna go off when he sees that empty room."

"Right and I hope the son of a bitch starves to death."

"Rainy, if Roger stole all that money, you know he has more. He wouldn't put it all in one place."

Actually Rainy had not thought about that. The thought was disturbing. "You may be right but we just couldn't sit and wait for them to come back."

"I know, just scared is all."

"Which way we going?" Rainy and Sofia had climbed to the flybridge.

"Down the east side of Eleuthera and through Current Cut." Higgs nodded to a chart he had on the table. "Think if El Conquistador is motoring back from fishing around Bimini they will stay outside the Bight."

"You gonna call Roger?" Rainy and Sofia sat on of the settee.

"Yeah, figure he might give me a hint about where they are fishing. Could help us avoid 'em."

"Good idea."

Higgs picked up the mic. "El Conquistador, El Conquistador, this is the Catch 'Em whiskey tango alpha four, niner, five, zero, channel 16, over."

Almost immediately there was a response. "Catch 'Em, Catch 'Em this is El Conquistador, go to 68."

Higgs made the adjustment from the hailing/emergency frequency to channel 68. "El Conquistador, El Conquistador, need to talk to Roger, over"

There was a pause and Rogers voice crackled over the speaker. "Higgs, you got our package? Over."

Talking on a marine radio is not private so Roger and Higgs had kind of a code. "The package has been delivered. When is pick up? Over."

"Fishing north east of Bimini. Should be at dock in 2 more days. Call back if any problems with storage. Over."

"Understand. Catch 'Em, whiskey tango alpha four, niner, five, zero out."

"El Conquistador standing by channel 16."

"Well maybe we got a couple of days to make it to US water. Keep the radio off. No contact. Don't want them to hear from this boat." Higgs instructed.

"So I'm a package in storage huh?" She glared at the radio. "Can we make it?"

"Should slip by 'em if they are catching fish and stay up to the north east toward Freeport. Never know when they might chase a fish somewheres else", Higgs pointed at the chart. "Soon's we get into the Florida Straits, think we'll be free of 'em. You know how to steer?", Higgs asked Rainy.

"Never have, 'bout you Sofia?" She shook her head no.

"Gonna have to learn a bit, you are. Can't do all of it 'cause we need to run all night."

Rainy and Sofia got a quick lesson on watching a compass heading and using the auto pilot. The boat had state of the art gear and really was easy to keep on course. The main variables were weather and the Gulf Stream.

"Look we've passed the stone crab buoys and shoals so I'm gonna get some sleep. Just stay alert. The autopilot will do the work. If another boat gets too close, disengage and throttle back. Just stay out of their way." Higgs left the women on the flybridge.

"Shit girl, this is crazy. I guess we'll just watch for other boats like he said. Want me to bring up some coffee?"

"Yeah, think I can handle it for now." Rainy looked around. "Not a boat in sight."

Soon Sofia came back with a thermos and a couple of mugs. "Still nervous, but glad we are doing this."

"Yeah, better than sittin' around."

"So, how did you get Higgs to come? By the way is that his first name?

"Not sure. Have heard the Higgs name all over the island, so think it is just what he goes by. Anyway, I told him we would sell Catch 'Em and he could have half."

"Good deal for him if you can sell the boat."

"Come on Sofia, it won't matter." She rolled her eyes.

"Oh yeah." Sofia laughed. "Hard to believe how much this boat is worth right now."

"Uh huh, so let's pay attention. Sure don't want to sink her."

They motored on through the Bight of Eleuthera. Hours later Higgs came up to the flybridge. He stood for a moment looking at the gps plotter and gauges.

"On course, good." He indicated for Rainy to get out of the captain's chair.

"You want us to fix some coffee?" He nodded and they went down to the galley.

"I think I could eat. How about you?" Sofia opened the fridge. "Sandwich?"

They made one for Higgs and Rainy took it and a thermos of coffee to the flybridge.

"Brought you something to eat too." She sat the thermos and sandwich on the chart table.

"That works for me. You girls might want to get some shut eye. I'll stay up and get us past the Biminis."

In Rainy's cabin the women undressed and got into the double bed. At first they slipped together, kissing and fondling frantically driven by mutual attraction and fear. Exhaustion quickly overcame their sexual urges and they fell asleep.

On the flybridge Higgs watched the gauges and the compass. So far this had been a pretty easy job. He knew it was really out of character for him to do something so spontaneous. Stealing the boat didn't bother him, but taking off with these two weird women had the markings of drama and disaster. The reward would be worth the risk if they could sell the boat. He began to think that he might even just stay in Florida. He had piloted boats over many times before but was always pulled back to the cult-like life in Spanish Wells.

Since his brother was killed though he had been thinking it was time to break away. How odd that Roger apparently killed Freddy Brovania de Maurice, the man that killed his brother. Of course Freddy had denied it and blamed it on a local girl named Sarah Sweeting. The court agreed but ran Freddy out of the Bahamas. The last time Higgs saw him was as The Baron left the shipyard in Spanish Wells. Now he was dead too.

Since Higgs decided to run all night he was pretty sure he could avoid El Conquistador. Roger had no reason to be looking for Catch 'Em. Higgs had not said it was repaired, so unless they passed within eyesight there should be no problem getting to US waters.

By law, he was supposed to check out of the Bahamas and pay an exit fee. As a commercial fisherman he had skipped that little bureaucratic exercise many times. Getting into a US port could be trickier. He knew from past trips to avoid the large busy ports where they would be boarded and inspected. The US Coast Guard and Border Patrol didn't have the manpower to be stationed at the many inlets up and down the Florida coast. The marina he was going to was known to be slack about paperwork for the right bribe. Once the Catch 'Em was tied up he could lay low until Rainy found a buyer.

Chapter 25

Wilbur Bonnet handed his backpack to the mate and his new drinking buddy Squiggy. He stepped down into the cockpit of the Dawn Lee. The sun started to break the horizon. Squiggy introduced the other three men that would be fishing with him on this makeup charter. The boat's captain was on the flybridge and had the engines running. As soon as the dock lines came aboard they were off.

Wilbur sat in the fighting chair as the other men disappeared into the cabin and went back to sleep. He watched the water change shades as they got further away from land. He was hopeful that today he would finally catch a big fish. Even if they didn't, he thought he could get used to this lifestyle. Fishing all day and having a few drinks at night was far better than dealing with slippery crooks, small town politics and budgets. He got out his camera and took a few pictures of some of the commercial fishing boats that were also heading out for the day. He was well prepared to capture the action if they caught a big fish. He had developed an interest in photography many years ago when his police department was able to buy a really good camera for crime scenes. Now he owned the best equipment he could afford.

After about two hours of running, the captain of the Dawn Lee pulled back on the throttles. Squiggy climbed down from the flybridge and began putting out lines. The change in the engine tone woke the other anglers. Squiggy explained that each man would sit in the chair for thirty minutes at a time. Whatever fish was hooked that man would fight then rotate out for the next angler.

"You guys figure out what order you want to fish in." Squiggy said.

Wilbur volunteered to go last. So the other men picked the three remaining slots. As often is the case when trolling, most of the time is spent waiting and watching the baits bob around in the wake of the boat.

As the Dawn Lee trolled toward Bimini from the west, the El Conquistador was dragging lines from the east headed for the same fishing grounds.

Aboard the El Conquistador, Roger could see that Luis' mate knew what he was doing. He had local knowledge which had already helped avoid uncharted shallows. He also expertly prepped the trolling rods and rigged the baits. When they reached the fishing ground he knew just by the shade of the water and signalled for the captain to slow up. He quickly got the lines out. Now they were fishing.

Roger wasn't thrilled to sit on the flybridge of Luis' boat instead of his own but he felt excited about the possibility of catching another big marlin. He also thought it strange that he had so much passion about a hobby. He never felt this way about anything else except his airplane. He had even murdered Captain Freddy without a thought. Well, he didn't care.

Luis joined Roger on the flybridge. He was a strange little man and was a non-stop talker. Normally Roger would have no patience with endless chatter but for some reason he liked the sound of his Dominican accent. So he just listened to Luis babble about the sky, the water, the birds and how the baits were performing.

On any given day there are many boats trolling the waters around Bimini. A lot of fish stories begin with "We was dragging lines near Bimini...". Actually Bimini is a chain of islands located about fifty miles due east of Miami. It consists of North Bimini, South Bimini and East Bimini. It is an area of myths, legends and lies.

Roger could see boats in every direction. Luis cautioned his captain to stay as far away as possible. "Cross lines, it'll be a mess." he pointed to one boat that was particularly close. "That guy is hooked up. Fish could run any where, give him wide berth."

On the Dawn Lee, Wilbur had just gotten out of the fighting chair when the reel sang out from a strike. He had to just watch as the next angler fought an as yet unseen fish. He cursed under his breath. So far this had been the only bite and he had been in the chair twice. He climbed up to the flybridge to get out of the way and have a better view.

The captain of the Dawn Lee was on the radio telling the other charter captains he was hooked up. He also was cursing a boat that he thought was too close. "Got a god damn googan about to fuck up my lines."

Wilbur looked over at the boat that had pissed off his captain. He noticed it had a uniformed crew and was named El Conquistador. He saw a tall bald guy scramble down from the flybridge. The man in the cockpit, obviously the mate rocked back on the trolling rod setting the hook. Then handed it off as the tall guy got in the chair. Wilbur cursed again. Seemed like fish were all around when it was not his turn.

The captain of the Dawn Lee radioed to the El Conquistador to watch out because he was hooked up. The boat didn't respond.

On the El Conquistador it was like a fire drill. A marlin had come up into the baits and the mate dropped back and hooked it. He shouted for Roger to get into the chair and the fight was on.

Marlin are generally solitary fish. They don't school. Though sometimes a male and female will pair up. This was one of those times. The Dawn Lee had hooked the male and the El Conquistador had the female which are always larger. The fish knew they were in danger and tried with all their considerable strength to swim to each other. This was causing the boats to get too close as they ran with the fish.

As the action got more frenetic Wilbur got his camera from the cabin. While he was aggravated that he was not the angler he realized how rare it was to see one marlin caught much less two on side by side boats.

The captain of the Dawn Lee was yelling at the El Conquistador to move away. The captain steered with the fish that Roger was fighting and Luis yelled back for the Dawn Lee to yield.

Below the ocean's surface a life and death struggle was playing out. The female marlin was over fourteen feet long and weighed more than a thousand pounds. The male about ten feet and a little less than seven hundred. While sport fishermen and scientists were puzzled about marlin mating and family habits, it was quite simple to them. They hunted together. They protected each other. They procreated. Now apparently they would die together.

The big female sensed the male was nearby. She swam hard. She jumped, she tail walked, she shook her head trying to dislodge the hook. She emitted some kind of panicked signal to her mate. He was trying to close the gap between them too. He charged through the water and rocketed upward, spinning, rolling and flipping. Then he dove deep as did the female. Some instinct taking them down into the dark cold depths.

The Dawn Lee and El Conquistador were no more than twenty five yards apart now. Both lines were straight down. The chaos of a few minutes before seemed to take a break.

"Think we got us a pair! Means they will try to get close to each other. They do and we lose 'em!" The Dawn Lee captain yelled.

The mate of El Conquistador agreed. He had heard tales of a pair being hooked by one boat on two lines but being hooked by side by side boats was a new one.

"What 'cha got in mind, captain?" Luis yelled.

"You turn south, I'll go north. Try to force 'em apart before they wrap our lines."

Luis nodded and his captain turned the wheel. The El Conquistador's bow slowly moved south. The Dawn Lee turned north.

The boats now were stern to stern still only about twenty five or thirty yards apart.

"Roger that fish is gonna come straight up when it feels the pressure. Be ready to reel." Luis yelled down from the flybridge.

Just then a bulge in the surface burst in a blur of iridescent blue and ocean foam. Both fish came soaring out of the water simultaneously. They hung in the air sizing up their enemy and disappeared into the same hole. Everyone saw the lines were wrapped and tangled.

"Go to neutral!" The Dawn Lee captain yelled to El Conquistador as he pulled both throttles back. "God damn. You gonna have to cut your line."

"Fuck you, cut yours!" Luis challenged.

Wilbur captured all the action on his camera from the flybridge. He again was disappointed he wasn't one of the anglers but he knew he was witnessing something special. Ironically, Roger was thinking as he waited for his fish to jump again that no one from his little home town of Frostville would believe this tale.

Now each angler was tied to almost two thousand pounds of raw fury. Neither boat was willing to cut their line. There was all kind of danger in this situation. The boats were too close, the two fish together exerted more power than one man could possibly reel in, any mechanical malfunction could cause a collision, sinking one or both boats, and who knows what else could happen. Marlin have rammed boats and even impaled fishermen. Their spears are four foot weapons of destruction. But the stubborn fishermen were obviously not going to yield.

The fish went deep again. In the lull before the next action, Wilbur swung his camera toward the El Conquistador. He wanted to record this rare event from all angles. Since the boats were still stern to stern the camera lens was focused right on Roger. Wilbur could see the intense concentration on the angler's face. Just then the two fish began to come up again. Roger picked up the rod tip and reeled hard. Without realizing it his face was in full view of the camera. Some gut reaction in Wilbur made him stay with the shot. He recognized Roger!

The fish again exploded through the surface. Both came up only a few feet from the El Conquistador's stern. The mate was startled and stumbled backward falling to the deck. Roger had no where to go. The two fish slammed the transom with their full weight. The male slid off to the port side of the boat. The much larger female's spear came half way up over the stern and impaled Roger right in his face!

There was a momentary pause and then the heavy fish slipped backwards into the water dragging Roger with it. The mate scrambled to his feet and grabbed for him but he was gone. Just gone. Wilbur gasped but kept filming. The guys on the Dawn Lee were at the stern looking into the water. Nobody jumped in.

The captain of the Dawn Lee saw what happened. He shouted for his mate, Squiggy to throw a life ring overboard toward where Roger had disappeared. When the ring hit the water it automatically activated an EPIRB (Emergency Position Indicating Radio Beacon). He came off the flybridge and actually jumped into the water. When he did, the El Conquistador mate went in too. They dove under but immediately knew it was futile. The weight of the attached rod and belt would have taken Roger down even if he wasn't mortally wounded from the stab in the face.

Squiggy told the man that had been fighting the male marlin to reel in to see if it was still on the line. He did but the fish was gone. Mother nature had definitely won this round.

Wilbur and Squiggy pulled the Dawn Lee captain out of the water. Luis came off the flybridge and helped the mate climb back on the El Conquistador. They rafted up the boats side by side. The activation of the EPIRB would bring swift action.

"God damn! Ain't never seen nothing like that." The Dawn Lee captain stood in the cockpit drying off. "Had people fall overboard before, but could rescue 'em pretty quick. That fish looked like it meant to kill that man."

"A freak thing, it was." Luis offered. "Been 'round the water all my life, know shit can happen but ain't never seen nothing like that. What we gonna do now?"

"Gotta wait for the Coast Guard. I called to tell 'em and they want us to sit right here. So was that guy the owner of the boat?"

"No, I'm the owner." Luis said."He was a guest."

Wilbur had been listening to this exchange and his police mentality kicked in. "Think we should notify the man's next of kin?"

"How we gonna do that? All I know is his name was Roger." Luis shook his head. "Met the guy in Bimini. His boat had problems so invited him to come along."

"So where's his stuff? Must be some ID or something." Wilbur climbed over to the El Conquistador.

"Don't know that you oughta be messing around with his gear."

"Well, we got time to kill and I'm a cop. So unless anyone has a better idea, I'm going to look." None of the men objected so Wilbur entered the salon of the boat.

Luis followed him. "He was staying in the guest cabin on the port side. I'm coming with you."

"No problem. Ain't gonna steal nothing. But that guy looks like someone I know. You say his name was Roger?"

"Yeah, Roger's all I know."

Wilbur knew he had no jurisdiction and since he was retired he wasn't technically even a cop but he was sure Roger was Harvey Hall from Frostville. He might have been bald and beardless but when Wilbur looked straight at his face through his camera he knew it was him.

He opened some cabinets and pulled out a few drawers. He found some neatly folded clothes. In the bathroom a passport was stuck in his shaving kit.

"Here's the guys passport." He carefully opened it so if there were any finger prints they would be preserved. "Can see he entered Bimini on August 15. Says he's American. Name of Dan Willis from Danville, Virginia. Thought you said his name was Roger?"

"Well, that's all I ever knew him by." Luis said.

"Curious. It says he was five feet four and had brown hair. That Roger guy was over six feet and bald and this picture don't look much like him either."

"You know, what did you say your name was?" Luis was getting upset.

"My name is Wilbur Bonnet."

"And you're a cop you say?"

"Uh huh."

"Look, you may be who you say you are but this is my boat. So let's go topside and wait for the Coast Guard. Let them sort this mess out."

"No problem."

When Luis turned to leave, Wilbur pocketed the passport.

The radio on the Dawn Lee crackled and the captain answered. It seems the Coast Guard was handing the accident over to the Bahamas Defence Force because the signal buoy indicated the boat was in Bahamian water. The instructions were to wait for the BDF.

"Not good." Muttered the captain of the Dawn Lee. "Have dealt with the BDF before. It will be a pain. Might as well settle in, it will take 'em hours to get here. No sense of urgency, this bunch."

The Bahamas Defence (yes, it is spelled correctly) Force mostly patrols the Bahamian water for immigration and poaching violations. Their equipment is no where near as modern as the US Coast Guard and their personnel are woefully under trained. When the patrol boat finally showed up at the site, the officer in charge had no idea what the situation was. Communication from the BDF home base was sketchy. So it took a lot of explaining to get the story of the incident understood. Even if there had not been an educational and cultural barrier, the fact that a fisherman died when he was stabbed by a marlin is difficult to believe.

Fortunately, Wilbur's video captured the bizarre occurrence. The BDF captain suggested strongly that the Dawn Lee and the El Conquistador follow him to Bimini. This meant the boats would have to clear Customs on Cat Cay. The Dawn Lee captain objected because as an American vessel he would have to pay the fees for entering and leaving the Bahamas, overnight accommodations plus lose the next day's charter. The BDF officer was stumped. He did not think he could force the American boat into a Bahamian port since this was essentially an accident investigation.

Wilbur Bonnet had been in law enforcement for his whole adult life. He intuitively knew that this unusual situation had the potential to escalate. He addressed the Dawn Lee's captain and the BDF officer.

"Captain, I suggest that I go with this officer and his crew. I have the video and am an eyewitness. I don't mind spending the time as long as I can find my way back to Islamorada in a few days." He looked at the BDF officer who seemed to be considering his offer.

"Do you have your passport?" The officer asked.

"I do." Wilbur handed it to him.

"I think this might be a good idea. Now, the El Conquistador came from Harbor Island, is true?"

Luis nodded and reminded the officer that his captain and mate were Bahamian citizens. "If we could just go back to Harbor Island, it would save an overnight in Bimini."

"This too makes sense." The officer nodded again. So this is a good plan. Take the El Conquistador and this gentleman to Harbor Island and we will come to see you in a day or two."

Luis looked at Wilbur. "Works for me."

The three boats separated. The Dawn Lee headed west back to Islamorada with no fish but one hell of a tale to tell. The BDF patrol vessel headed south on another call. The El Conquistador went east for the long run to Harbor Island.

Wilbur sat on the flybridge passenger seat while the mate steered the El Conquistador. Luis leaned against the rail. He chattered on about how strange it was to see a man killed by a marlin. He also wondered what would become of Roger's possessions.

"I mean he has a boat and a cottage on Spanish Wells." But Luis was really excited about Rainy. He was already planning to lure her onto his boat.

"Well, the man didn't just fall out of the sky. He must have some family somewhere." Wilbur added.

"Yeah, maybe but when we were drinking I got the feeling that he was pretty much a loner. 'Course lots of guys that come through these islands are running, ya know? He does have a girlfriend." Luis sensed he needed to fill Wilbur in.

"Yeah?"

"I met her. She knows my woman from when they both lived in Key West."

"Well she should know more about him." Wilbur was thoughtful for a minute. "Could see this would be an easy place to get lost if you had a mind to. Guess you just need a wad of cash."

"Seemed Roger had that. Paid a chunk for his boat and got a cottage over on Spanish Wells."

"What's Spanish Wells? How do you know all that?"

"Spanish Wells is fishing community not far from where I keep my boat. Its a small gossipy town. Everybody knows everything. The boat yard manager is my mate's cousin. Roger gave him enough cash to get the Catch 'Em, that's the name of his boat, to the head of the line for an engine refit. So, everybody knew that this Roger guy was spreading a lot of money around and was always in a hurry."

"He sounds like a man on the run." Wilbur stood to stretch. "You say the name of his boat is the Catch 'Em?" Luis nodded. Wilbur immediately saw the irony.

"How much longer?"

"About three hours."

Chapter 26

Late that night El Conquistador's captain throttled back as he entered the channel to Harbor Island. The change in engine noise woke Wilbur up and he climbed on to the flybridge where he found Luis too.

"Not far now."

Wilbur nodded. "How long do you think it will take for the BDF to come interview us?"

Luis and the captain laughed. "No telling. They won't be in a hurry. But you should spend some time here. You might like it."

Even in the dark the island seemed quaint and peaceful.

The captain backed the El Conquistador into the slip. The crew cleated off the dock lines.

"Coffee Shop's right around the corner." Luis pointed across the marina. "I'll meet you there in the morning and we can go over to Spanish Wells and find Roger's girlfriend to tell her what happened. Stay on my boat tonight." He climbed down to the dock and walked away.

Wilbur sat in the fighting chair and thought about the day. His police mentality catalogued the events as if he would have to repeat them in court. As far as he could tell this was simply an accidental death. There didn't seem to be any motive to kill Roger except from the fish of course. It was just trying to save its own life. Strange to witness though.

He moved onto the couch in the salon and watched the video again. When the shot was directly on Roger's face he froze the frame. He was ninety nine percent sure Roger was the fugitive Harvey Hall that he had been chasing for so many years. He decided that he would not reveal what he knew since he didn't know if Luis or the girlfriend were involved in the fraud.

He pulled out Roger's passport to see if there were any visa stamps that might give him a clue to where else Roger had been. There were no other stamps but In the back sleeve he discovered a single key. It had no markings. No way to know what it was for. He puzzled over it for a while then stretched out on the couch and went to sleep.

A jarring noise from the deck woke Wilbur. He opened the salon door and saw Luis looking over the stern.

"What's going on?"

"That bitch is gone." Luis was very angry.

"What bitch?"

"Sofia! My woman! She ain't in my condo. I think she must be over with Rainy."

"Rainy?"

"That's Roger's woman! Going over to Spanish Wells to see." The crew lowered the retractable swim platform and slid the Zodiac into the water. "Come on."

Wilbur wasn't sure what he was getting into but he grabbed his backpack and climbed down into the small boat. One of Luis' crew had the engine running. As soon as he was on board they took off.

The sun wasn't up so Wilbur couldn't see much. He didn't know anything about these islands but in ten minutes the boat edged into a large boat slip.

"God damn Catch 'Em's gone." Luis grumbled. "Could be at the boatyard, I guess. Come on." He jumped over to the dock.

Wilbur followed and caught up as Luis crossed the street and headed up the walkway.

"This Roger's house?" Luis grunted and banged on the door.

"Pretty early, ain't it" Wilbur knew from his police experience that unexpected visits sometimes were dangerous.

"Yeah, Roger's dead so.." he didn't finish the sentence but opened the unlocked door and went in.

"Sofia? Sofia?" Luis looked around and then climbed the stairs. The bedrooms were empty. There were open drawers and some clothes on the floor. Back down in the kitchen the cabinet doors were open and cans of food strewn about.

"Looks like someone ransacked this place." Wilbur observed. "What do you think is going on?"

"Can't be sure. Thought I would find Sofia over here laying up with Rainy."

"Oh." It was all Wilbur could say. "So you think someone robbed this place and took these two women?"

"Don't know." Luis sat at the kitchen table.

"There's some kind of building out back." Wilbur was looking through the kitchen window.

They found the workshop door open and turned on the lights. Inside the sex dungeon theme caught Wilbur completely off guard. "What the hell is this place?"

Luis was looking around at the St. Andrew's cross and the erotic art. "This Rainy woman was pretty rough. Guess she was into S&M. Ol' Roger too, I suppose." Luis sounded a bit wistful.

"What do you think is down there?" Wilbur was looking down into the dark storage room. Luis threw up the box switch and it lit up.

"There's a ladder, I'm going down."

"Anything?" Luis asked.

"Some empty storage racks is all." Wilbur climbed back up. "Let's go look through the house again."

They found some men's clothes and remnants of Rainy's wardrobe. Nothing to indicate who they were. Wilbur thought about DNA but even that was problematic. He couldn't see the Bahamas Defence Force going to the trouble on the request of a retired cop from North Carolina. He decided he would hang on to Roger's shaving kit and passport though.

"You said Roger owned this place?"

"Think he rented it." Luis said.

"Well there must be some kind of lease."

"Maybe, but things are pretty casual around here. You could ask around. Someone might tell you something but these people are pretty tightlipped. I'm going back to my boat. You coming?"

"If I don't, how do I get back?"

"To Florida?"

"Well yeah."

"Take the ferry over to Eleuthera and you can pick up a ride to the airport."

"Coffee shop?" They were crossing to the boat slip.

"That way." Luis pointed and jumped down into the

small boat. "Not sure what the fuck is going on but I'm taking my boat outta here." Luis' crew turned the Zodiac and motored down the channel.

Chapter 27

Wilbur watched the small boat disappear into the predawn darkness. It didn't sit right that Luis felt no responsibility or urgency to report the two women missing. He had to decide if he wanted to get involved in something he didn't understand.

The sun was coming up so he turned from the boat slip and walked along the neatly kept sidewalk. He liked everything he saw. The town was clean and each small cottage was painted either white or a bright pastel. It was reminiscent of a New England village.

The coffee shop was the 'Coffee Shop'. No Starbucks or Dunkin Donuts or fancy name. When he stepped inside the conversation stopped. The locals already knew who he was and had been jawing about the accident.

"Hey, have a seat." A weather worn man offered. "The place is buzzing this morning. No one can believe a man got killed by a fish that warn't no shark." Wilbur slid into the booth as a waitress put a mug of coffee in front of him.

"How do you know about that?" Wilbur poured some cream in his coffee.

"You kidding? All over the radio. Onliest thing anybody's talking about, it is. You on the boat?"

"Nope but I saw what happened."

There was a murmur from the nearby patrons and they edged closer. Wilbur took a sip of coffee and looked at the eager crowd. "Well, don't know what was said on the the radio but I've got proof that he was killed by a fish."

Wilbur got out his camera and attached it to his computer. People crowded around. They gasped when the marlin exploded out of the water and rammed its spear into Roger's face. Some looked away as the fish dragged him overboard.

This was the first time Wilbur had seen the action on his laptop screen. He had shown it to the BDF officer on the camera's small viewing panel. The larger picture showed the violent details of Roger's death. He played it again for some new arrivals

"Any of you folks know this man?"

"Know his name was Roger. Lives in the Pineapple House or he did." Wilbur's boothmate said.

"Did he have any relatives here?"

"Don't think he had any kin from 'round here. Had a woman. She's a looker."

Lots of the audience laughed. A few agreed. "She has a big tattoo of her face on her shoulder." The waitress said. "She comes in sometimes. Nice lady. Didn't bother nobody."

"Anybody seen her lately or know her last name?" Wilbur was asking questions like a cop.

No one spoke up.

"May I see that video again?" A well dressed man in the crowd asked. Wilbur played it again.

"My name is Godfrey Higgs." He put out his hand to Wilbur they shook. "My brother worked some for this man Roger."

"What did he do?"

121

"He ran Roger's boat. They fished together. What's your interest in all this?" The man sounded a bit officious so Wilbur was cautious.

"Well besides seeing him killed, I'm supposed to wait for the BDF to interview me."

Godfrey Higgs laughed. "Planning to be here awhile, are you?"

"Nice place from what I've seen but need to get back to Florida soon. Your brother around?"

"Well, I haven't seen him lately. I might be able to help you out."

"How so?"

"I'm a barrister. What's your name?"

"Wilbur Bonnet."

"I could take your statement for the BDF. Might save you some time."

"Might be a good idea. Where's your office?"

Godfrey Higgs pointed out the shop window. "Just there." He paid his tab and left.

After some breakfast and a few more showings of the video to late comers, Wilbur left the Coffee Shop and walked across the street to the lawyer's office. 'Godfrey Higgs, Attorney at Law' was stenciled on the large window.

Inside the furniture was from the 1940's. Dark paneling covered the walls that were hung with law degrees and portraits of Higgs men, in the wigs worn by British barristers. Godfrey Higgs came around the desk and put out his hand to Wilbur. "Have a seat." He pointed to two wingback chairs.

"So this was a strange accident."

Wilbur got out his camera and and showed Godfrey the clip again.

"Most remarkable. I have never seen anything quite like that." Godfrey had a British accent. "As this man, Roger Bannister's barrister I feel some responsibility to settle his affairs."

"Bannister you say is his last name?" Wilbur smirked. "As in Sir Roger Bannister?"

"Ah yes quite a coincidence, don't you know?"

"Well the passport I saw said his name was Dan Willis. You represent him and don't know his real name?"

"A puzzle, it is. However we often have people visit this island who want to remain incognito, as it were." Godfrey sat back in his chair. "I helped him rent the cottage where he was living."

"Since his death was an accident do you think there will actually be an investigation?" Wilbur asked.

"The video seems all the proof one would need to close the books. Unless a relative comes forward to demand further action or some kind of insurance claim is made."

"How would a relative or insurance company even find out about the accident?"

"Good question but I am thinking that the BDF might want to see your video again.

"I suppose." Wilbur nodded.

"So, I propose that I represent you."

"To do what?" Wilbur looked puzzled.

"Well, to deal with any investigation that might come up. You don't want to let this newsworthy video be shown for free, do you? If the BDF gets it, you can be sure it will also make it to the media."

"Never occurred to me. But there is someone who would know more about this Roger guy."

"Of course, the woman with the tattoo." Godfrey said. "Well now, this does change some of what we know but not much. I suppose I should have a chat with her."

"Not sure she's still around."

"At any rate Mr. Bonnet you might still need representation."

"I guess. How do you get paid?"

"I will draw up a contract. I get paid a contingency fee only if I negotiate a deal to your satisfaction."

Wilbur wrote a statement about the accident that Godfrey Higgs notarized. Also, they agreed on percentage split if a video deal was negotiated.

Wilbur now had an attorney, uh barrister. Together they would negotiate any offers that came his way for the video. He also thought he would try to find Godfrey Higgs' brother.

Wilbur decided to explore the Pineapple House again. He really had no right. His thirty years of police experience had put him in many situations that were only semi-legal. So his story if anyone questioned him was that he just trying to help find a relative for the dead man. He had told no one that he suspected Roger Banister to really be Harvey Hall.

The front door was unlocked. Inside he found a very well built house that he really hadn't noticed during his earlier visit with Luis. There was a lot of crafted detail such as crown molding and chair rail over hand carved wainscoting. He kneeled to study the intricate wood floor.

"Made of basillito wood. Once abundant on these islands but now used up." Godfrey Higgs walked in the front door.

"Nice place, looks old." Wilbur moved toward the kitchen.

"Yes, built by one of the original settlers a long time ago name of Sanderman. Roger was only renting as I said. Man name of Basnight from up on the Outer Banks of North Carolina owns it. He's the third owner. He inherited it. Married a local girl but they never much use it. Not sure you should be in here."

"Well I'm a cop and I feel responsible for finding out if Roger had relatives. Place looks ransacked."

"A cop you say?"

"Well, retired. On vacation. That's why I was on that fishing boat." Wilbur's explanation seemed to satisfy Godfrey Higgs. He didn't reveal that he had been in the house with Luis.

They looked around and Wilbur didn't see anything that he might have missed that would shed more light on Roger's identity.

"I guess I will have to contact the owner and let them know what's going on. Normally my brother takes care of the property."

"Is this the brother that ran Roger's boat?"

"Yes, bit of a jack of all trades."

"Think I could talk to him?"

"Just heard he and that Rainy woman left out on the Catch 'Em. Quite disturbing. I am hoping that there might be something in this house to identify her."

"You mean your brother stole Roger's boat?"

"Not sure that's the way I would categorize it."

"What is your brother's name?"

"People around here just call him Higgs to distinguish him from me."

"Do you know where he might have gone?"

"Since his brother was killed not long ago, he has been acting a bit irrationally. He could be easily influenced by a woman."

"So there is no way to know where they went?"

"Well, I would say Florida."

"Why?"

"Because that's where everybody goes."

"Yeah?"

"Easy to get into even if you aren't completely legal."

"Do you think the US Coast Guard would help find them?"

"Based on what?"

"Well, your brother stole Roger's boat."

"You don't know that. This woman Rainy might own it and hired Higgs to run it like Roger did. No the Coast Guard is not going to look for them."

"So, they are just gone?"

"If they want to be. Why do you even care?"

"Just curious."

Wilbur Bonnet and Godfrey Higgs searched through the house looking for some kind of clue as to who Roger and Rainy really were. Everything looked the same as it did the night before to Wilbur.

Godfrey Higgs raised an eyebrow but really didn't comment about the sex dungeon except to say it looked like it had been wrecked. So all they knew was Roger was dead, his boat was gone and Rainy and Higgs were on it.

"Well Mr. Bonnet please stop in before you go back to Florida just in case I hear from my brother or discover anything else about all of this."

"Yes I will. Probably stay another day or so." But Wilbur was thinking he needed to get back to Florida. He figured if that is where Rainy went then that might be where the money Roger stole, or what's left of it, went too.

Chapter 28

Higgs had no trouble bringing the Catch 'Em across the Gulf Stream and into Old Cove Marina just below the Lorelei Tiki Bar and Marina in Islamorada. He did a deal with the harbormaster and was rented a slip with no questions asked. Once the boat was tied up it looked like any other transit yacht with a For Sale sign in the window.

Rainy was back in her element. She had spent more than a decade hustling for a living in the Florida Keys. She wanted to show off her new found wealth.

"I'd kinda like to flaunt this money. Show all those assholes that looked down their nose at me." She and Sofia were sitting in deck chairs having a drink while Higgs was up in the marina store buying more beer.

"I know what you mean but might want to lay low for a while. See if Luis or anybody's chasing us. You know Roger did try to hire Higgs to fuck you up. Might've hired somebody else. If you flashing some coin, they might find you."

"Yeah, you're right. See it all the time. Some bunch of rednecks pull off this great job then go right out and buy a ton of bling and fancy cars. Gets 'em caught every time. We do need to figure out what to do with all the cash though and get rid of this boat. Could just buy a house and move."

"Or another boat."

"Now that's a good idea." Rainy stood and caressed Sofia's shoulders while kissing her neck. "Trade this boat or sell her outright and buy another one."

"Think we could run it?" Sofia stretched her arms and caressed the back of Rainy's thighs."

"Look at all the dumb asses that have boats. Think we could do fine. Don't need one this big though. I used to live on a houseboat, probably find one in Key West."

"What about Higgs?"

"Don't know. He's a funny little guy. Pretty harmless I think. He might just want to hang here for a while. Get away from that stupid island."

"Yeah who knows. Right now though I got other plans." The two women caressed their way down to their cabin.

The next day Rainy met with a man that was interested in buying Catch 'Em. She was asking $240,000. The man wasn't quibbling on the price but wanted to arrange to have the boat documented. This would involve paperwork and ultimately an inspection. She knocked another $25,000 off the price for a quick no doc sale. The man was a bit sketchy too and understood the situation. He would pay $200,000 for an 'as is' deal the next day. Now Rainy had to find somewhere to move the hidden money.

"Gonna go find us a car." Rainy didn't tell Higgs she had a deal. She left Sofia on the boat just to keep an eye on things and hiked out to US 1. She knew there were car dealers all along this stretch.

Rainy dropped $21,000 on a late model Malibu because it had a large trunk and was candy apple red. It wasn't fancy but she was thrilled. She had never owned a decent car and she had never paid for one in cash. The sales woman got all the paperwork and temporary tags done without any hassle. In fact she told Rainy she would jump in the car and 'run away in a skinny minute'. Lots of women and men just couldn't resist her.

That evening when Higgs had gone up to the Lorelei Tiki Bar, Rainy and Sofia loaded the cash into the car.

Over coffee the next morning Rainy filled Higgs in on the sale.

"Yeah, the man is coming back with cash."

"Damn, how much?" Higgs poured some cream into his mug.

"Just what I told you. So your half is one hundred thousand."

Higgs shook his head in amazement. He never figured this job to work out. "Guess we ought to celebrate some."

"Nope, not till the cash is in hand and we still need to lay low. Roger could be looking for us."

"Thought you said he wouldn't come back to US water."

"Did, but he might have hired somebody to look for me like he did you. He's got to be pissed. So we do the deal then get as far away as we can. What you gonna do?"

"Not sure but don't want to go back to Spanish Wells. Ain't never had any money before so might just hang around Florida for a while."

"Well one thing.

"What's that?"

"Need you to take 'Catch 'Em' off the transom. The

buyer ain't gonna want that name and no sense making it easy if somebody's looking for us."

"Not a problem."

Chapter 29

Wilbur spent the night in a B&B in Spanish Wells. He found the local watering hole called the Little Bar and drank with some of the people he had met in the Coffee Shop. He had to tell his fish story quite a few times. He tried to get some information about Roger and Rainy but found out very little at first. Roger had come in frequently. He bought rounds and mostly talked about fishing. People knew who Rainy was but she kept to herself the few times she came in.

One woman had spent time with her. She was the very attractive wife of a fisherman. She only reluctantly talked to Wilbur out of earshot of her husband and after a few drinks. She said Rainy basically picked her up in the Coffee Shop by telling her she was an artist and needed a model. The fisherman's wife was bored and flattered. She went along to the studio behind Roger's cottage. The woman said at first she really did pose for a portrait that became a nude painting. She went back each morning for about a week. She said she found it very exciting. When the painting was done Rainy gave it to her. The next day she brought it back because she knew her husband would not approve. She told Wilbur she and Rainy spent that morning loving each other. She blushed and looked panicked. She said she didn't know why she was telling Wilbur this but she was worried because she had tried to find Rainy for the last several days and she was just gone. She didn't know Rainy's last name or anything else except she was a pretty accomplished artist and had come over from Florida.

Wilbur decided to go by the attorney's office and then head to the airport. He was thinking now that Rainy took off when she found out Roger was killed and probably has what was left of the stolen money. At least she might know something about where it was. The Joint Interagency Task Force had determined that twenty to twenty five million was stolen. So Wilbut figured some of it had to be unspent. Anyway he wanted to get back to North Carolina and have the DNA from the shaving kit tested.

"Mr. Bonnet do come in." Godfrey Higgs opened the door to his office as if expecting Wilbur. "I saw you coming down the walk. Lovely day, is it not?"

"It is. I just wanted to let you know I am flying out today."

"I see." Godfrey moved behind his desk and sat. "Please have a seat."

Wilbur really didn't want to get into a long conversation so he stood. "I really need to get to the airport but just wanted to check in to see if you knew any more about Rainy."

"Well I have found her to be quite the proficient artist and shall we say seductress." Godfrey seemed a little embarrassed. "Contacts have let me know that her nude art is very highly regarded and the subjects were quite enamored of her skill, if you get my meaning."

Wilbur decided to sit. "So she painted nude models and then seduced them?"

"Apparently. No one complained. It seems most of her subjects were wealthy women but there were also a few locals."

"That is helpful I think," said Wilbur.

"Still not sure why you care." Godfrey Higgs was suspicious.

"Well don't care enough to chase her but am curious to know what she knows about Roger since I did see him die." Wilbur did not trust the barrister enough to fill him in on who he thought Roger really was and about the money he stole.

"I see. Well that does bring us to the video. A news journalist from Nassau made contact with me. She heard about it from a relative here."

"Who was it?" Asked Wilbur.

"Well the mate from the El Conquistador was recounting the story over in the Glass Bridge bar and this reporter's relative works there."

"Did she offer to pay?"

"I assured her of its content and she said she would get back to me," said Godfrey Higgs.

"Well if she does, you can negotiate. Then contact me and I'll send her a copy."

"What if she wants an exclusive?"

"For the right price, I can give that up."

They shook hands and Wilbur walked to the ferry just in time to get on. After a short ride to the dock in North Eleuthera he got a ground taxi to the airport. While he waited for his flight to Ft. Lauderdale he thought about what he had learned by sheer coincidence in the last few days.

He was 99.9% sure Roger Bannister was the fugitive Harvey Hall. He was 100% sure he was dead. He had a shaving kit that he was sure contained DNA to confirm Roger's identity. He had a passport in the name of Dan Willis from Danville,

Virginia and a key of some sort that might be a lead as to how Harvey disappeared and where the money might be. He knew this Rainy woman had lived with Roger and could have some of the stolen money. He knew she was a tall, fit woman with a tattoo of her profile on her shoulder and a proclivity for rough sex. He knew men and women were attracted to her and that she was some kind of artist. The woman from the El Conquistador was known as Sofia and probably Dominican. Finally, he knew he loved Florida and the Bahamas and wanted to return.

Chapter 30

Rainy rented two rooms at the Islamorada Resort which was just across US 1 from the marina. She gave Higgs one of the keys and told him to meet her and Sofia at happy hour over at the Lorelei Tiki Bar. She then went back to the Catch 'Em to close the sale. The man didn't show. Rainy waited for an hour. She was a little freaked out. She kept her hand on the .38 Smith & Wesson in her bag. It was the one she had stolen from Freddy.

She knew the local culture and deals rarely went down as planned or on time. She didn't have any way to contact the man since neither had exchanged names or numbers. She decided to go back to the hotel room and discuss what to do with Sofia.

When she got to the hotel room Sofia was waiting anxiously. She hugged Rainy.

"I was so scared. I was sure this was a bum deal."

"Well the guy was a no show. Think we ought to give him another day. Ya know?"

"Yeah, shit happens. If he doesn't show, what?"

"Well, thing is we got plenty of cash. Could just give Higgs a hundred thousand and be shuck of him."

"How do you explain where it came from? I mean if he knows you got so much he might want more."

"You're right. Think I could just tell him the deal went down. He don't need to know nothing else. He gets his money, he'll be happy."

"Yeah, good idea. What about the boat?"

"Fuck the boat. It got us here, shit we can just leave it. Higgs already sanded down the transom and my names not on it. Just leave it here."

"You're right."

"So we'll meet up with Higgs, give him the money and tomorrow head out."

"Damn you're a smart sexy woman. Come here."

Wilbur flew to Ft. Lauderdale. He had left most of his clothes and gear in the Islamorada Resort when he had gone off fishing to Bimini on the Dawn Lee. He was anxious to have the shaving kit tested but decided that a few more days in the Florida sun was more important. So the trip back home to North Carolina would be delayed. After all Roger wasn't going anywhere and the possibilities of finding Rainy were slim. He really only had a general idea what she looked like. He thought he might even go out fishing again. He rented a car and drove the two hours south to the hotel.

Squiggy had finished cleaning up the Dawn Lee after a pretty good day of fishing and generous tips. Now he was looking forward to a cold beer. He dodged some tourist traffic on US 1 and walked into the Lorelei Tiki Bar and climbed up on his favorite stool. Lately he had become a minor celebrity because he was a witness to a marlin killing a man. He rarely had to buy a drink anymore. He relished his little bit of fame and embellished his story with his heroic effort to save the fisherman.

Wilbur got to Islamorada just in time for happy hour at the Lorelei. He parked the rental car at the resort and walked across US 1 and entered the popular bar. Almost immediately he spotted Squiggy holding court for some eager sunburned tourist fishermen.

"Tell ya, been fishing all my god damn life, ain't seen nothing like it. Almost like that big ol' marlin was after that man!"

Wilbur listened as Squiggy told his story. Essentially it was true but like all fish stories got better with the telling.

"Couldn't save the man, tried my damndest but that fish just took him down, I was, God damn! This man saw it too. He was on our boat!" Squiggy had spotted Wilbur and hopped off his stool to put his arm around him. "Get this man a drink. Damn man, warn't sure I'd ever see you again."

Rainy and Sofia walked into the Lorelei wearing beach cover ups over their brief bikinis. Mostly fishermen tourists from the charter boats came in to drink cheap rum and swap lies. Not many women braved the alcohol and testosterone fueled bar. The women were ogled and whistled at but no one had the courage to actually approach. They found Higgs sitting by the window in a booth and joined him.

"Higgs, guess we can do a little celebrating." Rainy smiled.

"No shit? Got cash?" Higgs was about to jump out of his skin. "Be right back, first round's on me." He slid out of the booth and made his way through the crowd to the bar. As he stood waiting to get the overworked bartenders attention he heard Squiggy retelling his tale to a new group.

"That god damned monster fish came over the transom like he was hunting the man what hooked him." Squiggy paused for effect and looked around at the excited crowd. "Then it jammed its spear right into Roger's face!" He slapped his hands together for emphasis. The crowd sucked in a collective breath. "The fish was fourteen feet if it was a fucking inch. Over twelve hundred pounds, I reckon. Kilt ol' Roger instantly and pulled his body and the fishing gear right back into the water. We was stunned, I tell ya! Time we could jump into the water they was gone!"

The crowd just looked at Squiggy in awed silence.

"Bullshit!" A craggy looking old salt hollered from across the bar. "Ain't never believed that horse shit Squiggy. Who the fuck was this guy anyways?"

"Roger caught that big damn marlin a few years ago with Captain Freddy. That there's him." Squiggy pointed at the framed picture of the Florida record hanging over the bar.

"Yeah ain't seen him since and ain't seen Freddy neither. All bull shit!"

God damn it Joe, you warn't even there." Squiggy looked ready to fight then he remembered Wilbur. "This man was. Hell he even has a video of it."

"It's true." Wilbur said quietly. He didn't like to be the center of attention.

"I believe it when I see it." Said Joe.

They kept arguing until Wilbur said that he would bring the video tomorrow.

Wilbur looked at the picture hanging over the bar's cash register. He had seen it when he first came to Islamorada. He didn't recognize the angler as being Harvey Hall then because the man had his hat pulled down over his face. Now he could see it was him. He had shaved his beard and head since that photograph. Harvey Hall was Roger, he was sure of it.

Higgs looked at the picture too but he just saw a bearded man with a hat pulled over his face. He wasn't sure if it was the Roger he knew. He brought three drinks back to the booth where Rainy and Sofia were waiting.

"You hear that story?"

"Yeah some of it, sounds fishy to me." Rainy laughed at her little joke and Sofia smiled. "You believe it?"

"Seen sailfish jump right into the boat. Sos guess a big marlin could. Thing is, did you hear the name of the man what died?"

"Uh uh, too far away"

"Said the man's name was Roger."

Chapter 31

A dominatrix, a street whore and a fisherman walked out of a bar. The noise in the Lorelei had risen to that drunk incoherent level you hear at the end of tropical happy hours. They crossed US 1 and settled in lounge chairs around one of the resort pools so they could talk. Out of earshot of the other tourists they discussed the possibility that the man killed by the marlin was the Roger they knew.

"What are the odds?" Sofia wondered.

"It would be fucking fantastic if that asshole was killed by a fucking fish." Rainy was worked up. She got up and went to the outside bar and brought back more drinks.

Higgs was quiet. He was trying to figure out how to find out if it was Roger without tipping anyone off about where they were.

"Could radio my cousin at the marina there on Spanish Wells."

"Yeah but if Roger ain't dead, somebody gonna tell him you called in. He might got some of his creeps looking for me right around here." Rainy was getting drunk. "This is where we met. He used to fish with Freddy. Same guy what you said killed your brother."

"So you know people 'round here?" asked Sofia.

"Yeah, that guy telling his goddamn fish story is Squiggy. Mate off some charter boat."

"Then he probably knows who you are?" Higgs asked.

"Fuckin' doubtful." She threw back a shot. "Couldn't afford my sweet ass." She laughed.

"Yeah, but would know you if someone was looking."

"Don't think he would recognize me. Cause I ain't lookin so fine as I did."

"Just saying, we need to get out of here is all." Sofia nodded in agreement.

"Hear that, but want to know if that asshole Roger is dead."

"That Squiggy fella said some other guy had a video that showed the whole thing. Was gonna show it tomorrow. Guess we could wait around to see it."

"Uh huh, makes some sense. Yep, thass what we do." Rainy laughed.

Later, Wilbur stumbled back across US 1 to his hotel room. He rarely drank more than a few beers, but he had gotten caught up in Squiggy's storytelling excitement and even added a few details for the audience. He drank the free shots the fishermen sent over. He flopped onto his bed and was about to go to sleep when he noticed the message light blinking on the phone. It was Godfrey Higgs asking for him to call back. Wilbur decided to wait until morning.

Over room service breakfast and a hang over Wilbur called the attorney. He learned the newspaper had made a

substantial offer for exclusive rights to the video and an
interview. The deal was for Wilbur to download the video and
send it to the newspaper in Nassau after a deposit had been made
to his attorney's escrow account. Wilbur was shocked that he
would receive $10,000 minus Godfrey Higgs' fee. The exclusivity
clause meant that the newspaper could sell copies to other news
services to recoup and if it went viral, make money. In that case a
percentage would also go to the escrow account. Wilbur was
admonished to keep the video secret. If he showed it and word
got back to the newspaper they would take back the money.

In spite of his massive hangover, Wilbur was excited. He
didn't care that he had promised he would show the video at the
Lorelei. He just wouldn't because this windfall would allow him
to stay in Florida longer. He decided to check out and drive to
Key West. A place he had always wanted to visit. On his way he
would stop at a UPS store and send the shaving kit back to the
police station in Frostville. Then he would have one of his
buddies get it tested against the DNA they had on file for Harvey
Hall.

It was very early and Rainy was awake. She never slept
well after drinking too much. She was jittery and paranoid that
her car and money were gone. She grabbed her keys and slipped
out without waking Sofia. Dressed in gym shorts, a loose tank top
with no bra and flip flops, she walked down the three flights of
steps. It would be faster than the elevator and she would be less
likely to run into any other resort guests.

In the parking lot she immediately saw her car and felt
better. She was about to go back up to her room when she saw a

guy messing around near the trunk. She watched for a few seconds trying to decide what to do. Then walked across the lot intending to just get in the car and drive off. As she got closer she could tell the man was at the open trunk of the next car over. He was just trying to gather the stuff that had fallen out of a suitcase.

She decided to move her car anyway because she wanted to open the trunk and assure herself that the money was still there. As she unlocked the driver's side door she spotted a can of shaving cream that obviously had rolled away from the hapless tourist and lodged under the front wheel of her car.

"Hey mister, this yours?" Rainy came around the back of her car.

"Thanks, having one of those days." He looked sweaty even this early. Rainy smiled then got in her car and drove around the building to a parking spot she would be able to see from her room. She opened the trunk and was satisfied that the money was undisturbed. She stared at the neat bundles for a few seconds and for the first time wondered who Roger stole it from. She quickly shook off that thought and slammed the trunk.

Wilbur recovered his wayward things that had fallen out of the unzipped suitcase when he lifted it off the luggage cart. He finally got it all together and shoved it into the trunk. He had a blinding headache but something else gnawed at his brain. He couldn't bring it into focus though. He started up the car, turned left out of the parking lot and headed south on US 1 toward the Conch Republic.

Wilbur found a UPS store in Marathon about forty five minutes later. He bought some packaging and sent the shaving kit on its way to Frostville, North Carolina. He had already alerted a friend in the police department to get the kit analyzed in the State Lab. Wilbur asked his friend to keep his suspicions a secret until there was definite evidence about Roger's identity.

Chapter 32

Most of the people that Harvey Hall had ripped off had gotten on with their lives. Those who had lost their homes were still struggling, but had long ago given up on finding Harvey and bringing him to justice.

Barbara Hall had left Frostville. While never officially charged in Harvey's crimes she was the target of vicious rumor and innuendo. Deserted by her country club friends, her kids were taunted in school and she could not find a job of any kind. With her parents help, she went to live with her cousin's family in Virginia for a fresh start.

Lawsuits and counter lawsuits against the mortgage bank, the bank officers, the development company, the general contractor, the insurance company Harvey represented and Harvey were still working their way through an overburdened court system. After over three years most were losing steam for lack of money for legal fees.

All of the mess was still a hot topic of conversation around Frostville. In the spring the town council debated whether or not to remove the 'Harvey Hall Baseball Complex' sign on the Little League field. The trouble was no one had stepped up to pay for a replacement. The same was true at the 'Harvey Hall Gym' at the high school.

These reminders and 'Harvey sightings' kept the story alive. At first they were weekly, now every few months someone would swear they saw Harvey on a tropical beach somewhere. Ironically, up until the fish attack these sightings could have been true.

Now by some strange coincidence Wilbur Bonnet may have found Harvey. Or at least his ghost. Also, without knowing, he was within inches of some of the millions of dollars Harvey stole. If he had not been so hungover and flustered when a very sexy, sleep-tousled woman handed him a can of shaving cream, he would have immediately recognized Rainy from the tattoo on her shoulder. As it was, this vital visual clue was bumping around in his throbbing head. He stopped for coffee.

Chapter 33

"The fuckin' boat is gone!" Rainy slammed into the hotel room where Sofia was just waking up.

"Huh? What?" She was naked and sat up against the headboard.

"The fuckin' Catch 'Em's not there." Rainy pointed across the street. "Motherfucker came back and stole it!"

"That sucks, but do you really care? I mean we stole it too."

Rainy thought for a minute then burst out laughing. "So funny that I don't give a shit about a quarter of a million bucks...but I don't." She climbed into bed. "Now if you were gone, I'd be pissed." They kissed for a long time.

Rainy and Sofia lay on the bed as their sweat streaked bodies cooled. "Let's go jump in the pool." Rainy got up and wrapped herself in a towel.

"Rather you do that again." Sofia smiled.

"Then we go for a swim?"

The women put on brief bikinis and decided the ocean was better than the pool. In the clear, cool water the morning's lovemaking got a fresh start.

"Damn girl you are going to drown me if you keep that up, I can't breathe"

Rainy laughed and disappeared under the water.

At happy hour, Rainy and Sofia dressed down in almost identical oversize t shirts, modest cut off jeans, flip flops, baseball caps and big sunglasses and entered the Lorelei Tiki Bar. Anyone that had seen Rainy previously would not have recognized her. They ordered drinks and mingled with the fishermen tourists. The hub bub was the usual stuff about fish caught and the one that got away. Cheap rum and beer were disappearing in huge quantities. Higgs was sitting at the bar.

Squiggy entered like a celebrity. Claps on the back guided him to his stool where a couple of beers were waiting. He held one up, "Fishermen!" he hollered and the reply was a bunch of unintelligible grunts and encouragement to tell 'the story'.

The crowd was just as enthusiastic as ever because almost every day at least half were newbies that had just arrived to fish. Old salty Joe again challenged the veracity of Squiggy's tale. It was supposed to be settled by Wilbur's video but he was no where to be found so the argument just blew up. This time Squiggy and Joe came to blows and the bartender threw them out to the drunken jeers of the happy hour crowd.

"Looks like we ain't gonna find out anything about Roger. Let's get out of here." Rainy said. She could sense that even dressed down as they were, the horny fishermen were noticing her and Sofia.

"Hey Higgs we're going to Key West if you want a

ride." Rainy said as she passed him.

"Yeah" He climbed off the bar stool.

They crossed the highway to the resort. "Get your stuff and meet us at the car."

Fifteen minutes later they were heading south.

"So Higgs, I know you've been over here but ever been all the way down to Key West?"

"Nope, was gonna a while back. Just didn't."

"How come?" Rainy was just making conversation.

"My brother got kilt. We was gonna do it together."

"What was his name?"

"Higgs. He the one that Freddy kilt."

"Higgs? Is that a first name?"

"Nope."

"How many Higgs are there?"

"Bunch. Kinda like all of George Foreman's sons being named George." He laughed.

"I think that's the first time I've heard you laugh."

"Well, hell. Got money in my pocket. It's a good day."

"Hear that. Listen, how do people know which Higgs they was talking about?"

He laughed again. "Just do."

"Well still having trouble believing Freddy killed your brother but I'm sorry for you."

"It's okay. He was getting crazy. Think that's what that island does. Figure on not going back."

"Yeah? Well just so you know Key West is a crazy island too."

Higgs just nodded and they rode on in silence.

Chapter 34

Wilbur's hangover slowly dissipated as he drove down US 1. He had read about the construction of the Florida East Coast Railway by Henry Flagler. He recalled that there were forty seven bridges. He was crossing some of the remaining concrete arches installed in the first decade of the twentieth century that were now supporting the highway. When he crossed the Seven Mile Bridge he felt like he was driving on a very long pier. The water was that Caribbean turquoise that no one can quite describe. He did wonder about the hardships the men that built the railroad bed went through. He had read that many of the workers down here back then were WW I vets and quite a few died.

They must have been desperate was all he could think. One summer he had done construction work in Frostville which certainly wasn't in tropical heat through a mosquito and snake infested swamp. After that job he decided to become a cop. He figured chasing bad guys and even getting shot at was a better gig.

Wilbur had a loose plan. He would be a tourist in Key West and since he was looking for Rainy it gave him a reason to check out the town and ask questions. He figured her name and evidently her unusually sensual appearance, and profile tattoo would make it pretty easy to track her down if she were even in Key West. Of course, he had absolutely no authority to do police work here in Florida. Except if he could make a connection to the fugitive Harvey Hall he thought he might be able to get help from the local cops.

While the sight of so much turquoise water was awe inspiring, it soon became a bit monotonous and Wilbur's energy needed a boost. Near Sugarloaf Key he saw a sign for Baby's Coffee and pulled in.

The smell of roasting coffee perked him up. Inside he was warmly greeted and welcomed to the Conch Republic. He saw the nation's flag with the motto " We seceded where others failed" that celebrated the 1982 rebellion.

Wilbur ordered 'Death by Coffee' from a friendly barista. Then wondered to himself if this should be to go. He chuckled at his little joke.

"So what happened in 1982?" Wilbur was looking at the flag.

"Well, I wasn't born. So what do you mean?" The young woman smiled earnestly. Wilbur decided to drop the subject.

"Never mind. Have you worked here long?"

"Yeah, little over a year.." Okay Wilbur thought, I have entered another universe where 'little over a year' is a long time.

"Ever hear of a woman named Rainy?"

"Sure, everybody know Rainy."

"Seen her lately?"

"Haven't. Strange too, 'cause she a regular. Good tipper too."

Wilbur got the message and put a five in the tip jar.

"Know her last name or where she works?"

"Nope." Wilbur could tell he had asked too many questions. He was in a foreign country and needed to learn the culture.

"Thanks, good coffee." He stuck another five in the jar and was rewarded with a beautiful smile.

Half a day behind Wilbur, Rainy drove her new Malibu south too. She had made this trip countless times but still was awestruck by the tropical beauty. The sun was going down and the light sparkled off the water. Sofia had fallen asleep but Higgs was wide awake. He was like a little kid on a field trip. He was not formally educated but Rainy sensed he was a smart man. At least he was smart enough to not hit on her or Sofia. In fact she sensed he was even a bit protective of them.

"You wanna drive?" Rainy was tired.

"Never have."

"Never?"

"Well ain't never had no need. Boats all I know."

"Key West is perfect for you. Don't need no car. Bicycle or scooter. Thats how most people get around."

"Think I can find work?"

"Lot of charter boats."

"Yeah, kinda sick of that."

"Everything else is tourist stuff too."

"Paint some, I do."

Rainy lifted an eyebrow in surprise. "Paint what?"

"Just what I see."

They rode on as the warm tropical darkness descended. Rainy began to think about what she was going to do in Key West. She always had to hustle before but now she had plenty of money. Maybe she could buy a building she and Sofia could live in and have an art studio. Hell, maybe Higgs might turn out to be a partner. She just wished she knew what Roger was doing. She hated that she had to look over her shoulder constantly. She knew he would kill her.

"Shit!" Sofia woke up with a jolt.

"What? You 'bout made me run off this bridge."

"Know how to find out if that guy the fish killed was Roger."

"Yeah, how?" Higgs perked up too.

"Simple, just ask what boat he was on."

"You're right! It would have to be the El Conquistador. So do you know how to call the boat?"

"Ain't hard." Higgs said. "Just get on another boat and use the radio. 'Course the son of a bitch would have to be in range."

"Got no love for Luis, huh?" Sofia asked Higgs.

"Asshole. Thinks he better'n me 'cause he got money."

"Uh huh, but Higgs if El Conquistador is in range that means they probably be headed to Key West." Sofia looked worried.

"True. Think he'd be looking for you?"

"Could be. He knows I been down here before. 'Course he a big sugar daddy and can get lots of girls."

"Why you girls fall for that shit?" Higgs asked.

"Can't speak for Rainy but just the way of Dominican women. I learnt from mi Madre who was kept by mi Padre who warn't her husband. She learnt from her Madre. If you lucky to look good, it's what you do. Didn't want to but only other work's on the street."

"You do that?"

"Ain't your business, but yeah. Damn near got beat to death by some pimp ass son of a bitch. So when I healed up I made it a mission to find me a sugar daddy. Most of 'em are drug dealers that make fast money. I lit out for Key West. Worked like a dog. Finally met old Luis, he already made his drug money. So I rub his back you know? Make him happy. Act like a true Dominican woman."

"What's that mean?"

"Cook, clean. Fuck him and swear he the best ever."

"What you get in return?" Higgs was downright curious.

"Get so much but lose so much. Dominican women be complex. Can be very strong but want traditional life. I got no education so my body's all I got."

"So Luis got plenty of girls?"

"Yeah, he got 'em and a wife and kids too."

Higgs shook his head. He had no idea about the world outside Spanish Wells.

"Look, if we call on a ship radio ain't we tipping off where we are?" Rainy was concerned.

"Yeah some but not exactly."

"But if Roger ain't dead his buddy Luis might let him know. Wait, I got a better idea." Rainy thought for a minute. "Why don't I call the Lorelei and act like a reporter and ask ol' Squiggy to tell me the story. Then I can ask him what boat the guy what got stabbed by the marlin was on."

They all started laughing. "Sometimes the simplest plan is the best." Rainy smiled.

Chapter 35

Wilbur was wandering around Mallory Square at the foot of Duval Street about an hour before the sun started to go down. The square filled up quickly with tourists and street performers. He doubted many locals joined in the sunset tradition unless they were hustling the tourists. So he was there for the entertainment. While he knew this celebration happened daily, he did not expect such a large crowd. Soon the street acts were set up in obviously designated spots. He heard one of the jugglers say he had been performing daily for thirty years.

The acts were as varied as a side show at a county fair. There was Dominique the Crazy Cat Man who trained house cats to do the kind of tricks lions would do in the center ring of a circus. He danced and sang to his cats in a mysterious accent. The fickle animals actually walked a tightrope and jumped through a hoop of flames.

There were jugglers, fire eaters, sword swallowers, escape artists and music acts. The mix varied some from year to year but not much. Everyone worked for tips so some were funny, some were insulting, some were arrogant. The tourists usually showered them with dollars.

Also, there were local arts and crafts for sale along with food and plenty of margaritas. The mass of people usually paused to toast the moment of sunset and clapped as if it was performing just for them. They lingered for a bit and then cleared out.

Wilbur enjoyed the festive atmosphere and indulged in a few drinks. He sat on the seawall and just watched the happy crowd. He wondered if Rainy might be near. He saw many stunning women in skimpy outfits. None that had a profile tattoo. Then he figured as a local she probably lost interest in this daily show long ago.

He was glad to witness the craziness. At fifty five he was beginning to think he really had not lived a very exciting life. With freedom and irresponsibility hanging heavy in the tropical evening he had the alcohol-induced epiphany of hundreds before him, *maybe I could find a job and just stay in Key West.*

Wilbur's cell phone vibrated. Since he had come back to the US he had turned it on. He recognized the number from the police station in Frostville. The conversation was brief. His buddy confirmed that the DNA in the shaving kit matched the DNA on file. The dead fisherman was Harvey Hall.

So after years of chasing false leads, Wilbur had found his man by pure coincidence. He had watched him die at the hands of Mother Nature. Now he was trying to track down a person who might have or know where the balance of the stolen money was. A story the media would have a field day with. Now he wasn't so sure he should have sold the rights to the video of Roger being killed.

Wilbur stumbled up Duval Street and climbed up onto a bar stool in Sloppy Joe's. He would worry about Harvey Hall, the stolen money and Rainy later. While he had never heard of the syndrome, he was experiencing Keys Disease.

Chapter 36

The "Fish Kills Man" video was getting a lot of attention. It was a local news story in the Bahamas but quickly was picked up by larger media outlets. It crossed over to the Internet and went viral. It was transformed from a serious news item to a bit on late night television. Saturday Night Live particularly had fun reviving their Landshark sketch using a marlin costume.

Squiggy was having his fifteen minutes of fame. Reporters were becoming common in the Lorelei Tiki Bar. They sat around and waited for him to finish fishing for the day then pounced as he came in for a beer. He was thrilled at first but the routine quickly got old.

The story was working its way down the Keys. It made for a good tale at the dockside bars. Since Rainy, Sofia and Higgs were on the move they were unaware of the increasing buzz about Roger's death.

At Mile Marker 15, they pulled into Baby's Coffee. The clerk was not the same one that waited on Wilbur so no suspicions were raised that anyone was looking for Rainy. Refueled with coffee they got back in the Malibu.

"Was thinking we'd check by the place I used to live. Might be a vacancy."

"Got room for me?"

"Higgs, you're okay. Sure. I used to live on a boat, so it will be right in your wheelhouse."

They all laughed.

"All right then."

Rainy turned off of US 1 which had become Roosevelt Boulevard and onto Palm Avenue. She pulled into a small marina on Garrison Bight. She parked just past a gaggle of scooters.

"I used to live on one of the house boats. Let me go check with the marina manager and see what's up. I'll be right back." She walked under a sign over the pier that said 'Owners and Guess' and climbed onto the first boat on the right. Whoever answered the door squealed in delight and pulled Rainy inside.

"Popular girl." Higgs observed. Sofia felt a little threatened. They got out of the car and wandered around.

"Think that's spelled right?" Sofia pointed to the 'Owners and Guess' sign.

Higgs shrugged. "Ain't much for spelling, but it don't look right."

Higgs knew right away that these 'boats' were liveaboards. He had never seen so many that were permanently berthed. "Guess these folks don't go nowheres," he mumbled.

"Right. When I lived here it was so expensive people were sharing anything," Sofia explained. "Sometimes even shared beds."

Higgs looked a little confused.

"I mean like if someone worked at night and someone worked during the day they just used the one bed between 'em. Hot racking its called."

"Oh, I heard of that. Navy thing."

"Yeah, think you're right. Pretty icky though."

"Icky?" Higgs laughed. "Do what you gotta do, I reckon."

"Hey guys." Rainy came up behind Sofia and Higgs. "This is pretty weird but one of the boats is for sale."

"Why is it weird?" Sofia asked.

"It belonged to a guy that just disappeared. The manager says no one had a claim on it so she's gonna sell it. Not sure how legal it is but I gave her some cash as a downpayment 'cause don't know what else we might find. So we can live in it until the ownership gets sorted out."

"Works for me. Which one?" Higgs looked out over the boats.

"Last one over on that finger pier," Rainy pointed. "Knew the guy. Local named Hugo. Used to do a cookout on Friday nights. Anyway, let's go check it out".

They went on board and were surprised to find it in good shape The manager of the marina told Rainy that the boat had been cleaned and was ready to rent or sell.

It had a simple houseboat lay out. A flat after deck led to a sliding door that opened into a salon. It had a galley, two staterooms and two heads. Up top was a deck for cook outs and lounging. It had shore power and minimal furnishings and the location was perfect. It was an easy walk or bike ride to everything in town. The engine had been removed for more storage. The boat would only be moved if a major hurricane was coming. Then it would be pushed by a tugboat to safer water. Essentially, it was a floating condo.

"Higgs, why don't you take the front berth, Sofia and I will take the one in the back."

Higgs got his sea bag from the car and dropped it on the bed. He climbed up to the top deck where Sofia and Rainy were sitting in a couple of plastic chairs.

"Its early, think I'm gonna walk around."

"Okay, just to let you know the whole island is about two miles by four so pretty easy to find your way. We're gonna settle in, maybe buy some groceries."

Higgs climbed back down from the top deck and walked off the pier. Rainy and Sofia watched him head down Roosevelt toward the center of town.

"Think we can trust him?"

"So far he ain't done nothing wrong." Sofia smiled and looked back at Rainy. "What do you think?"

"He might be okay. 'Course he don't know about the money. We need to get it out of the car. Think we'll hide it in the old engine room for now. Just have to see what Higgs is really like but he don't threaten me none and he ain't hit on either of us."

"Yeah, that's a little strange, don't you think?"

"Could be we ain't his type."

"Well, you're my type. Come here."

After Sofia and Rainy enjoyed each other they brought the money into the engine room from the car. Rainy squirmed through a hatch that was used to access the propeller shaft. Sofia handed down the bundles and Rainy stuffed them into the space.

"Safe enough for now, I guess. Sure would like to put it in a bank." Rainy said as she climbed out of the hatch. "Just not sure how to do that without bringing attention from the IRS or some other fucking government agency."

"What should we tell Higgs," Sofia wondered.

"Well, he thinks we have money from the sale of the the Catch'Em like he does. Guess we keep it like that for now. We'll figure something out. What time is it?"

"Almost seven." Sofia looked at her cell phone.

"You know what? I'm gonna call the Lorelei and see if I can get a hold of Squiggy. He's probably still drinking."

"Don't use your cell."

"Good point, I know there's a pay phone up by the office. I'll go use it then we can go find some food."

Rainy tracked down the phone number for the Lorelei Tiki Bar in Islamorada. When she got through, she identified herself as a reporter for the Key West News. The person that answered hollered for Squiggy. She could hear him ask who it was and the line went dead. She called back and the same person said, "Mr. Squiggy ain't takin no calls." He hung up.

"Well lets go get some groceries and think of something else."

While they were driving to Fausto's, Sofia said, "You know, I don't know nothing about you, 'cept you make me cum."

Rainy laughed. "What else is there to know?"

"Like, where you from? How'd you get down here? What's your last name. Stuff like that."

"Want to know my favorite color?"

Sofia smiled. "You're making fun of me."

"Okay, ain't much of a story. Originally from Ireland. Last name is O'Ryan. Came over when I was a young'un. My Dad got a job mining in West Virginia. It was a shit hole town and he was killed in a cave in when I was seventeen. My Mom lost it. She couldn't raise my three younger brothers and me, so I got on a bus. I rode two days and got off at the last stop behind the Dim Sum shop on Duval Street. I had landed right in the middle of Fantasy Fest." She laughed. "Thought I was on another fucking planet."

"How'd you make it?"

"Got a job waitressing pretty quick. But figured out the real money was in stripping if you got a good ass and firm tits. So, that's how I started. Made some good money and was doing okay till I got tangled up with a jerk. So listen I'll fill you in on the rest later. Let's get some food and we need to buy some sheets and towels."

Higgs found a barstool in Sloppy Joe's. He nursed a beer and absorbed the early evening atmosphere. He could tell that there was a hard core group of local drinkers at one end of the long bar. Tourists came in waves, wandering in and out. A rough looking skinny guy on the next stool filled him in.

"There are sixty some fuckin' bars on this street. God damn tourist wander up and down drinking till they get shit faced. Me? Sit right here and get shit faced. That walkin' stuff's too much fuckin' trouble."

Higgs just nodded. Same kind of drinking in Spanish Wells, just not so many people and fewer bars. He decided to wander though. He wasn't ready to be a hard core local drinker yet.

He noticed the crowd was quite different from back in the Bahamas. There it was either very rich or poor. Here there seemed to be all kinds of people. Rich, poor, young and old. Most were having fun. Just walking, drinking, eating and enjoying the tropical air. He began to think this place could be a good fit. He turned onto Greene Street and saw a bar called Captain Tony's. Inside, he immediately liked the vibe.

A block away, Wilbur was having pretty much the same feelings. He wasn't a hard core drinker but enjoyed wandering in and out of the bars. In the little town where he had been police chief he really couldn't go out for a drink. It was just the way it was. Don't drink, be in church on Sunday. It was not really a sacrifice because it was his way of life. Now, though he was enjoying this free and easy Key West lifestyle. He was thinking he might never go back to North Carolina. He saw a yellow sign for Captain Tony's and headed toward it.

Fausto's Food Palace is a Key West institution started by Faustino Castillo in 1926. He came over from Havana in 1910 and worked in the cigar business until he opened his first store in a restored house. Since then it has grown into the place to go for specialty foods. Past customers have included the likes of President Harry S. Truman, Tennessee Williams, Ernest Hemingway and Jimmy Buffett.

"When I lived here, I probably shopped three or four times a week in Fausto's." Sofia loaded the bags of food into the back seat of the Malibu.

"So, what did you do?"

"Worked in the bars. Got some action on the side. Didn't strip, but wanted too. Just couldn't work up the nerve." She laughed.

"You mean you could fuck 'em but wouldn't strip for 'em? Well you sure got the body." Rainy teased. "Probably coulda made lots more jack."

"I hooked up with old Luis when he brought El Conquistador into the harbor. When he left for Eleuthera, he took me too. Sofia blushed.

"Are you embarrassed? 'Cause it's true. You got a fantastic fucking body. Come here girl." Rainy pulled her into a hug. "Let's dump this stuff and go have some fun."

They put the groceries away then crossed Roosevelt Boulevard and rented a scooter. Rainy drove and Sofia hung on to her waist.

"We'll go to a bar I like and see what's going on." Rainy said back over her shoulder as she negotiated the narrow streets.

Rainy parked in front of a faded No Parking sign with a bunch of other scooters. They crunched across the oyster shell macadam onto a well-worn boardwalk where the day sailing fleet was tied up. They passed through a large open air bar restaurant jammed with happy people enjoying tropical air and umbrella drinks. Rainy led Sofia out the side door and up some stairs to a tower deck high above the waterfront.

"This is 'Slackers'. Mostly locals and one of my favorite bars. Ever been up here?"

"Nope." Sofia shook her head "Worked mostly on Duval. This is kind of cool."

"Food sucks but good place to get away from the tourons."

The women were not dressed provocatively. Both in shorts, t-shirts and flip flops. The trouble began soon after one of the local fishermen recognized Sofia from her days of working the bars. It wasn't long before a group of horny men were sending over drinks. In their working days, Rainy and Sofia would have accepted them with a smile and the hustle would begin. Now, it wasn't needed.

Clearly agitated Rainy said "Don't need this fucking shit. Let's get out of here." They crossed the deck to cat calls and whistles of the men and disappeared down the stairs.

Rainy turned and led Sofia out on a finger pier past the old turtle krawl. "I know about half of those guys."

"Yeah I do too," Sofia nodded. "Fucked most of 'em. Once a whore, always a whore." She had tears in her eyes.

They embraced. "Fuck 'em. We don't need 'em anymore." Rainy almost growled. "I got a plan."

"Yeah?"

Chapter 37

Quite a few Frostville cops had been burned in Harvey Hall scams so it was inevitable that the DNA results would leak. Once it was discovered that Wilbur Bonnet, retired police chief had found Harvey Hall, the word spread quickly through town and to the task force agencies. The initial burst of interest was dampened when no one could find Wilbur.

The resort in Islamorada where Wilbur was supposed to be staying while fishing was contacted. It was discovered that he had checked out three days earlier. The new police chief figured Wilbur was on his way back to NC since his calls went straight to voicemail. They would just have to wait.

Meanwhile, Wilbur was comfortably ensconced in the Sunshine Inn in Key West. He was enjoying the quirky little town and was losing interest in his search for Rainy. He loved sitting under the tropical foliage by the pool in the morning. His long years of responsibility did nag him a bit though so he decided that he would call back to the police station to check in. *Just as soon as he finished another cup of cuban coffee.*

After a few beers at Captain Tony's the night before, Higgs managed to find his way back to the houseboat. He woke up mid morning to the smell of coffee. In the galley he found a fresh pot and helped himself. Then he wandered up to the top deck.

"It is alive," Rainy joked. "How was your first night in this crazy town?" She and Sofia were sunning themselves in barely visible string thongs.

"Not like Spanish Wells." Higgs managed to sit on the foot of the Rainy's lounge chair without leering.

"Yeah, no place like this I've ever been. Think you are gonna stay?" Sofia asked.

"Yep. Some bar flies I met said I could make some money."

"Doing what?" Rainy reached back and undid her bikini top. "Put some lotion on my back." She handed the tube to Sofia.

Higgs didn't seem affected by Rainy's nudity. "Well, I told them I paint some, and they laughed and said the tourists will buy most anything if it is from Key West."

"Good to know." Rainy took note of Higgs lack of interest in her body. "You can set up an easel here if you want."

"I might but them local boys said to set up in that square where them big ships dock. Said new tourists come in most days. Just paint some sundown scene and tell a good story."

"Mallory Square. That's where they are talking about. Where the daily sundown thing is."

Higgs nodded. "Yeah, that's the place. Thought I'd find some supplies and give it a shot."

"Okay. We figure we'll just split the bills. Good for you?"

"Yep. How much I owe for the food and what not?"

They settled up and Higgs decided to go back into town to find an art supply store.

"Think Higgs is gay?" Rainy wondered.

168

"Why do you ask?" Sofia stood and stretched then lay on her stomach.

"Just never seen a man so uninterested in my fabulous bod," she laughed.

"He might just be smarter than most. Figures he's got a good thing and why fuck it up?"

"Yeah I guess. Don't matter. Seems he might work into my plan."

"Okay Rainy, that's the second time you've mentioned your plan."

"Well its not completely thought out but I want to start a business that puts the profits in some kind of program to take care of women like us. Think with all this money we can do some good."

"You are such a sweetheart." Sofia moved over to Rainy's lounge chair and gave her a kiss. "What kind of business?"

"Well, like Higgs, I can paint. If the tourists are as hungry for souvenirs as he thinks then we might be able to open a gallery. Also thinking we could use the space to help women."

"The tricky part may be finding a building. Remember the last time I lived here that most are owned by a handful of white guys."

"How do you know that?"

"Just pillow talk, you know. Some of the guys I used to fuck, they seem to have the juice in this town."

Rainy laughed. "We got the juice." She stood and preened her naked body. "Plus, we got the cash."

"Yeah, thing is though we gotta find out about Roger and Luis before you spread any of that juice around."

Chapter 38

Wilbur's phone call to the new police chief in Frostville stirred up a lot of excited confusion. He referred to the video and the word got out.

Townspeople saw it on the national news and online. If the rumors were true and the fisherman was confirmed to be Harvey Hall, the Frostville citizens were overwhelmed with feelings of satisfaction and frustration. Where is the money?

So Wilbur's thought of settling into a carefree retirement in Key West was over. The Joint Interagency Task Force was being reassembled and they wanted him to lead it. He was asked to fly back to Frostville immediately.

Once a cop always a cop. Wilbur dutifully returned and showed up again at the rented store front the JITF was using as a 'war room'. He found an energized room full of officials waiting to hear what he had discovered. He told them about the bizarre death of the fisherman who turned out to be Harvey Hall, aka Roger Bannister. The DNA from the man's shaving kit confirmed it. He explained that he had searched the cottage where the deceased had lived with a woman named Rainy. He described her from the second hand reports of the people he met in Spanish Wells. Told them she was last seen with a man from Spanish Wells named Higgs. They were on Roger's boat called the Catch 'Em. He said he felt she would go back to Key West but he had not seen her there.

The other piece of evidence was the passport that Roger was using. It was for Dan Willis, Barbara Hall's cousin from Danville, Virginia. The FBI quickly determined that he had died some years before but wondered if Barbara Hall knew more than she had let on. The thinking was that maybe this information would be useful in finding where the money was hidden. Wilbur did not reveal that he had found a key in the sleeve of the passport. It was the first time he had concealed evidence and he wasn't even sure why.

Barbara Hall was asked to return to Frostville from Virginia where she had been living with Dan Willis' family. She was reluctant because she was in the process of establishing a new life away from the Harvey Hall mess. She had gone back to her maiden name of Frost and did not want to return. She was persuaded with a subpoena.

"I don't know anything more than I did when you questioned me three years ago." Barbara replied when asked by the special prosecutor about Harvey's disappearance.

"Did he often leave you to go on business trips?" The prosecutor was a fresh law school graduate who had not been involved in the initial investigation.

"Do I really have to go through this again? You have my deposition and you are asking the same questions all over again. And yes, Harvey often took business trips. He flew to Asheville on his last trip before he disappeared. Or at least that is what he told me he was going to do," said Barbara Hall.

171

"What happened to his plane?" asked the prosecutor.

"As far as I know, the FBI confiscated it."

"How much money did he have?"

Barbara was on the verge of tears. "I don't have any idea. But he left none behind. You can check with the bank. All the accounts were emptied and he borrowed against our house which I lost."

"How about cash. How much did he stash for you?" The prosecutor was getting aggressive.

She shook her head. "Nothing."

"You are living with Willis' widow, are you not?"

Barbara nodded.

"Why was Harvey Hall travelling on Dan Willis' passport?"

"No clue. He's dead." Barbara was angry.

"That's all I have for now. Do not leave town."

Wilbur Bonnet had become a minor celebrity since he cracked the disappearance of Harvey Hall. He repeated again and again how it was just dumb luck that he had been on a boat near where Harvey was killed. His video had taken on a life of its own. So even though the original was in Wilbur's custody there were copies all over the internet.

The task force studied the video to confirm the image was Harvey Hall. They even asked Barbara what she thought. She teared up when she saw it. No one was sure at first if it was from seeing Harvey impaled by the fish or because he had ruined her perfect world. "That's the bastard." She repeated over and over and seemed to enjoy his brutal death.

The young Bahamian reporter, Kyla, who originally surfaced the video discovered the victim of the marlin had been identified as a con man who had stolen millions of dollars. She got permission from her boss to visit Frostville to pursue the story. She was looking for information to support her theory that her island country was harboring many fugitives. She realized she was probably stating the obvious but rarely would anyone in her government admit it. Crooks were a huge source of revenue and a tolerated legacy going back to pirate days. She felt this could be her first really important story.

Wilbur was under some obligation to answer questions from the reporter because it was her newspaper that bought his video. He didn't mind because he thought that he might get a lead about Rainy from the publicity.

Kyla and a locally hired cameraman interviewed Wilbur in the storefront being used by the Joint Interagency Task Force.

"How did you know that the man killed by the marlin was the con man that you were looking for?" Though Kyla was a native Bahamian she had been educated at Elon University in North Carolina and even had adopted a slight southern accent.

"I didn't know the man was Harvey Hall. I was videotaping the fishing action."

"So when did you know?" Asked the reporter.

"The man's face looked familiar. At first I didn't think much about it because as a cop I had seen hundreds of suspects."

"What struck you about this man?"

"I knew Harvey Hall. We lived in this same small town. I did business with him. I had been chasing him for years. So when

I really studied the video I just felt it was him. He had altered his appearance but I knew."

"Altered, how?"

"He had shaved his head and his beard."

"Did that make a big difference?"

"Well he had the beard and longish black hair as long as I knew him. A good looking guy, tall and fit. The change was dramatic in a way that if you really didn't know him well you probably wouldn't recognize him."

"So what did this Harvey Hall do?"

"Over time he stole millions of dollars from his friends and neighbors."

"How?" asked the reporter.

"Through a series of insurance and banking schemes."

"So how long did you chase him?"

"Well, about three years personally. Then I retired. The case had pretty much gone cold by then."

"How'd he get caught?" Kyla asked.

"Well, he never did. He ran. Well that's wrong, that big fucking marlin sure as hell caught him."

Kyla cut the interview because the last sentence could not be used. She asked him to be more careful.

The reporter then went on with background questions about Rainy and the boat, Catch 'Em. She ended the interview with an appeal from Wilbur as the leader of the task force for information. She closed with a shot of the artist's rendition of the tattoo on Rainy's shoulder.

Chapter 39

"He's fuckin' dead!" Higgs slid open the salon door where Rainy and Sofia were sitting at the table eating dinner.

"What? Roger's dead?" Rainy stood up.

"Yeah, just had a beer in The White Elephant down by the docks and it was on the news."

"We gotta get a TV. What'd it say?"

"This reporter from Nassau told the story. Said the man Roger what be killed by that fish was staying in Spanish Wells! Said his real name was Harvey Hall but went by Roger. Showed a video of him getting stabbed in the face!"

"Fuck me! Gotta be him then." Rainy and Sofia were jumping and hugging. "What else?"

"Said the man was some asshole crook what stole a bunch of money. I mean millions and disappeared."

Rainy and Sofia looked at each other. "Damn, knew he had money. Didn't know how he got it."

"Said fucking FBI and a bunch of other government fucks are looking for the money. Rainy, they looking for you!"

"What?"

"Yeah, used your name and had a sketch of you right down to the tattoo on your shoulder."

"Shit." Rainy and Sofia slumped onto the couch.

"Don't panic. Figure the worst we done is take a boat what Roger bought with money he stole. Hell for all anyone knows, he said you could use it. I mean, I was his captain you was living with him."

"So you think they are after me for taking Catch 'Em?"

"I reckon. What else could there be? You ain't stole that money from them folks in North Carolina did you?"

"Ain't never been in North Carolina." Rainy shrugged. "How'd they even know about me?"

"That guy what made the video. He a cop or he was. Retired or something but happened to be on that other fishing boat. He came to Spanish Wells and nosed around but we was gone." Higgs sat on the couch. "He's the lead investigator now. Wants to talk to you about where the money Roger stole is. You don't know do you?"

Rainy made a split second decision. "Look, you might not want to know what I know. That way, can't nobody accuse you of nothing. Okay?"

Higgs nodded. "We got money from the sale of the boat. But we gotta think this through. We tell that cop and they might make us give them the money for them people back in North Carolina. We gotta think," Higgs said.

"You know people around here ain't gonna turn me in to the cops or no Feds. That's just how Key West is."

"You believe that?" Sofia asked.

"I do. Most people here running themselves. But unless I stay hidden on this tub, I'm easy to find. Think we should up and leave?"

"Up to you. Do what you want. Could get another boat and head back to the islands. Stay lost there forever,"Higgs said.

"That ain't no life. Hiding out all the time. Okay Higgs I got to tell you." Rainy looked at Sofia who nodded. "Didn't get no money from Catch 'Em."

"What?" He looked up as she got up and paced around the cabin.

"Yeah, that fucker stole the boat."

"What fucker?"

"The guy that was supposed to buy it. Guess he figured since the deal was shady I wouldn't go to the cops. Yeah, so the money I gave you come from what Roger had hidden in the workshop behind the cottage there in Spanish Wells."

"Must be a shit load."

Rainy laughed and so did Sofia.

"You didn't have nothing to do with stealing it?"

"No, I said I didn't know nothing about where it came from and Roger never said."

"Shit, how do you know it was Roger's?

"Huh?"

"Coulda been from the family what owns the house. Lots of rumors about gold and money floating around that island."

"Higgs you're a smart man. Who the fuck knows? I mean, ain't it like finding gold coins at the bottom of the ocean? I mean that guy here in Key West that's got the museum, he found millions of dollars worth of treasure. It had to belong to somebody but he found it. Finders, keepers, I say."

"Still gonna be a rash of shit. Them cops are gonna try to prove you had something to do with Roger's mess."

Rainy liked that Higgs didn't ask where the money was. She decided he was a trustworthy man. "Look, think maybe you can help but if you want to walk away with the money I gave you, that's okay too."

"You been straight up fair with me so if I can help, I will."

"Cool. Well, think I need a lawyer?"

Sofia said, "Probably, but we gotta find somewhere else to hide the money."

"It's here?" Higgs asked.

Rainy nodded. "Agree with Sofia, them cops will tear this boat apart."

"So what do you think?"

"Split it up and hide it in different places. That way you won't lose all of it if they come searching."

"What do you mean? Bury it like some fucking pirate treasure?"

"Could, but probably not the best idea. If you hire a lawyer, couldn't he hold the money?"

"How about an offshore account? Heard Luis talking about that stuff all the time."

"Yeah but how do we get the money to an offshore bank?"

"Can't be hard to put it on a boat. Go to British Virgin Islands. Heard about guys doing that." Higgs offered.

"We need to talk to someone who knows about this stuff."

"My brother. He a lawyer."

"He a Higgs too?" Rainy smiled. Higgs nodded. "Where is he?"

"Spanish Wells. Would trust him with my life, I would."

"Good enough for me. Will you call him?"

"Yep." He got up. "Going up to that phone by the office."

"Should I go with you?"

"Can. Might have questions."

Godfrey Higgs took his brother's call. He was relieved to hear from him but quickly got on with the task at hand. He didn't need to know the source of the money to answer Rainy's questions. He described the steps usually taken to set up an account offshore. He cautioned that if there were tax consequences she should take care of them. "The IRS has longer arms than most agencies. Let's just say you won this money. So, it is income. Just make sure you pay the tax on it before trying to move it." Rainy got the impression that Godfrey had helped with this process more than a few times.

"A Cash Office may be the best way to go." Godfrey explained. "You won't need to set up an account. For a higher fee they will let you send the money instantaneously. In South Florida there are many of these operations. They routinely send money overseas."

"So can you handle things on your end?"

"I will set up a corporation and help you move the funds. I get a standard fee."

Rainy grinned to herself. *The man is so professional and polished. Hard to believe the short, rough man with a mop of tousled sandy hair standing outside the phone booth is his brother.* "Okay, I guess your brother has all the information I need to set up on this end."

"He most certainly does. If you have questions, phone anytime."

"Damn Higgs, you saved the day again." He just smiled.
"Let's do this before the cops show up."

Chapter 40

The special prosecutor continued to question Barbara Frost Hall. She was angry and hostile. He kept after her about the money she spent. He hammered her about where it came from.

"How much did you think a small town insurance agent could make?

"I raised our kids, I didn't work in the office. So I have no idea what kind of money he made. He always told me not to worry about it. So I didn't until it was gone."

"You took a trip to the British Virgin Islands did you not?"

"So? It was a vacation."

"Did you visit a bank while you were there?"

Barbara understood the implication. "I did not."

"Did your husband?"

She hesitated. "Can't remember. I was on the beach."

Wilbur sat at the table and watched the interrogation. He was sure that Barbara knew something. She could not have lived with the man and not known how much money was coming in and its source. Maybe she was in denial but he felt the prosecutor should keep asking hard questions. There might be some useful information about where the money was. He believed it was hidden somewhere.

"So you never saw your husband with a lot of cash?"

"I didn't say that. He always had it. I don't know how much. He just said he preferred to pay with cash. He hated credit cards and wouldn't let me have one."

"You didn't think that was strange?"

Barbara shook her head. "He paid the bills. I didn't care how."

"So he went around to all the stores and paid cash? Did he give you cash?"

"Yes, each month. He said that paying for things in cash would keep us out of debt."

"How'd that work out for you?" The prosecutor was being a jerk. Barbara started crying.

Wilbur left the conference room and took his Harvey Hall file to a desk. He just wanted to run through it one more time. He knew the details by heart but he always felt he was missing something in Asheville. He had gone there and met with the police chief when Harvey went missing. At first they thought it was a robbery and murder because some big real estate deal was on the line. Of course that later proved bogus.

The reference Barbara Frost Hall made to Harvey's propensity to only use cash posed a question. Did Harvey shuttle cash to Asheville on previous trips? Where did he hide it? This got Wilbur interested in checking out storage companies in Asheville. What he found quickly on line was that there were about a dozen storage companies but only one within walking distance of the Holiday Inn where Harvey was last seen.

Five hours later, Wilbur Bonnet pulled into Secure Storage in Asheville. This location was a block from the Holiday Inn. As the lead investigator for the J I T F, Wilbur was legitimately a law enforcement officer again.

The teenage clerk in the office was impressed with Wilbur's badge. Since he had no search warrant he just bluffed the kid. It took about fifteen minutes to determine which storage unit belonged to Dan Willis. It was being paid for by credit card with Barbara Hall's name on it and was up to date. *Yeah, she didn't have a credit card.* He knew she was lying.

The clerk got busy with another customer and Wilbur quickly found unit 106. He had the key from Dan Willis' passport sleeve. It fit easily into the heavy duty Yale lock. In seconds he was staring at ten heavy duty five inch Zero Halliburton Premier Silver Attache Cases. He knew what they were because he had busted a cocaine ring and these were the container of choice for cash. He just had to take a minute to decide what to do.

Chapter 41

Moving millions of dollars in cash became almost like a job. Rainy, Sofia and Higgs would load some of it into the trunk of the Malibu. They decided to only move a small portion at first and have someone always stay behind to guard the rest. They hoped to have it all wired to Godfrey Higgs before the feds found them.

They discovered there was an abundance of Cash Stores in Florida that would happily transfer funds for a fee. At first they visited a different store each trip, hoping to avoid too much attention. They didn't realize that most of these operations were owned by the same guy. Soon one of the managers pulled Rainy aside and told her for a little higher fee they could do all their transfers at one store and then she would not have to hopscotch around the county.

Rainy understood that this business was pretty shady but the money was getting through to Godfrey Higgs. She called him after each transaction. It was taking too long, though, and they were all worried about the FBI finding them and confiscating the money.

Rainy decided to split the money up. "What do you think? Do we hide some cash?"

"Why? If the feds find it, they gonna figure you or we had something to do with stealing it. Probably otta lay low for now." Suggested Higgs.

"I hear you, just feel like I want to know that if things go to shit, there is some cash nearby."

"Okay, you ain't talking about the feds now, are you?"

Sofia looked puzzled. "Something happened when you were here before, didn't it?"

Rainy teared up. "Yeah, don't wanna talk about it now. Just want to know if I have to run, I can."

Sofia and Higgs didn't need to know more. "Look, there must be a million places to hide some cash. Let's wire what we can, we'll hide the rest."

Rainy smiled. "I love you guys. I know exactly where we can put it too. After we take this batch to the Cash Store, I'll show you."

The dimensions of a million dollars are 8" x 6" x 13" in one hundred dollar bills. Higgs had the bright idea of stopping at Home Depot and buying some orange five gallon buckets, some tape and a shovel. They discovered that each would easily hold a million dollars and weighed about twenty two pounds.

"Now we just have to drive up to Sugarloaf Key to the place I want to hide these buckets." Rainy smiled. "Kinda like a pirate treasure."

"How you gonna find it again. All these Keys look alike?"

"You'll see."

At mile marker 17 Rainy turned onto a poorly paved road then stopped the car about a half mile down. Above them was a tall wooden structure.

"What the heck is this?" Sofia was out of the car and walking around the strange building.

"Its a bat tower."

"Been here a long time." Higgs was staring up the louvred side which was about thirty feet high.

"I read in one of those tourist pamphlets that it was built in the late 1920's so bats would live in it and eat the mosquitoes."

"Did it work?"

"What I read is that this guy named Perky bought bats from somewhere and released them into the tower and the next day the little fuckers flew away and never came back."

"One more island hustle." Higgs laughed. "All kinds of stories like that over where I'm from."

"So, you thinking to bury those buckets near here?" Sofia asked.

"Yeah, this thing has been here a long time and I figure if someone comes to visit it they won't be looking for buried Home Depot buckets."

"Pretty good plan. Damn, you're a smart woman."

"Gonna duct tape these lids before we bury 'em"

Chapter 42

At Secure Storage Wilbur Bonnet rented unit 108. He moved the ten attache cases to it and put his own new lock on the door. After closing up number 106 and securing it with Harvey Hall's old lock he drove back toward Frostville.

He was conflicted. He had rationalized that he had moved the cases to keep them out of Barbara Frost Hall's hand. Though for the first time in a long law enforcement career he was thinking about stealing the money. It occurred to him that only two people might know about the location. They were Barbara and Rainy. If either of them did know about the money and discovered the cases were gone who were they going to tell?

He decided that he would go back to Frostville and let the investigation play out. Then he could keep the money he had in storage and retire in style.

Since he was the lead investigator he really didn't have to explain where he had been. He entered the task force office and demanded an update from each of the agencies.

The Special Prosecutor reported that he thought Barbara Frost Hall was lying about what she knew concerning Harvey Hall's finances. Even though the SBI had found evidence of a joint credit card, he could not shake her from the story she told in her earlier deposition. They also knew Barbara had moved in with her cousin in Danville, Virginia.

The FBI did have a couple of leads on Rainy. They had an agent on the ground in Key West who was on her trail. She was only a 'person of interest' in Harvey Hall's misdeeds. They did not have enough evidence to arrest her. So the strategy was to observe and see what she was up to.

Chapter 43

Fortunately for Rainy the FBI had only discovered that she was well known in Key West. The undercover agent had not spotted her yet. So the money was buried before she was under visual surveillance.

Rainy kept enough cash on hand to pay for rent and food and to get her portrait business going. She decided to start with using the houseboat as a studio. She would lure tourists to sit for painting sessions like she did in Eleuthera. This time though Sofia would be present so she wouldn't seduce them.

"Don't worry girl, none of these women can make me feel as fine as you do. This will just be my attempt at legitimate art."

"You damn right none of those honky tourons are gonna ring your bell good as me." Sofia laughed. Higgs almost blushed.

"Yeah, anyways selling paintings is good cover for why you got money. Already found them tourists will buy pretty near anything made here on the island.

"Other thing is, I got my suspicions that somebody been following me," Rainy said.

"How do you know?" Sofia asked.

"Seen this woman a few times that's trying too hard to blend in. Just looks like a cop."

"Well, how hard would it be to find you? Ain't like you could hide what you look like."

"Is that a compliment Higgs?" Rainy teased.

"Take it for what you want." This time Higgs did blush.

"I wondered if you even noticed."

"Kinda hard not to?"

"Kinda hard?" Rainy had dropped back into her old bar hustling ways. "Just kidding you Higgs. You a good man and I appreciate that you don't hit on us."

"Learnt a long time ago that friends is more important than lovers."

"Wow Higgs, you are a deep man."

"Okay you two stop the bullshit. What do we do about this cop?"

"Shit, I say we live our lives. Ain't got nothin on me. If they did, I would be in jail," Rainy smiled.

At a small booth they set up daily in Mallory Square, Higgs would paint harbour views with the sun setting behind the Western Union which was an old sailing vessel that docked at the waterfront. The tourists snapped them up.

As he painted, he spun seafaring stories in his strange accent that sounded almost like an Irish brogue. He always drew in a crowd.

Sofia turned out to be an excellent salesperson. After all she had sold her body for years and selling art was a lot easier. She could spot the kind of vain tourist that would love to have her portrait hanging in her McMansion back home. She would show some of Rainy's work and make appointments for sittings. Soon all of them were too busy to worry about anyone looking for them.

The FBI agent who was observing Rainy quickly learned that she had two friends or acquaintances, a man and woman that seemed to always be with her. She saw the daily routine in Mallory Square. It was easy for her to follow and discover where they all lived. She reported to her supervisor what she saw. Her boss wanted more information so she made an appointment with Sofia to do a portrait.

"Rainy, I think I know who is trailing you." Sofia said as she unloaded art supplies from the Malibu.

"Really?"

"Well, this young woman asked for an appointment to do her portrait."

"Yeah, so?"

"She just ain't the type. I can spot the rich wannabes that can spend some jack to put their face on canvas. Usually middle age, heavy bling and have had work. Look tight now and want to preserve the fantasy. This girl, I mean she's young, wearing fuckin' long shorts, oversize T-shirt, dark skinned. Not the usual. Think she's a cop."

"She ain't gonna see much. Just a plain jane houseboat. She a cop, she figure spending some time sitting for a painting so she might trap me. Good work Sofia. Makes me pay attention. We'll just let her play her game."

When the agent showed up to have her portrait done, Rainy recognized her as the woman she had seen too often to just be coincidence.

"Hey, I'm Rainy. You must be Aleesha Morales." Rainy was reading from a form that Sofia had filled out.

"Yes. Nice to meet you." She stuck out her hand to shake. The woman was very formal so Rainy was pretty sure she was a cop."

"You here on vacation?"

"Well, kind of. Might be moving down here."

"People do it every day. Let's go up top where I've got my easel set up."

They climbed up to the second level where Rainy had created an outdoor studio.

Sofia was pouring coffee and offered Aleesha a cup.

"Let's talk a bit. We need to decide what you want."

Aleesha looked puzzled. "Not sure I know."

"Well, it's mostly a function of time. Some of my subjects are on vacation so they don't want to do too many sittings. If that's the case, I can take a few pictures and work from them. Some people only want a caricature. That only takes about a half hour. So, kinda up to you."

Aleesha seemed stumped for a moment. "I thought a portrait would make a good gift for my Mom. So, I don't mind doing several sittings."

She's pretty quick, Rainy thought. "Okay, tell me a little about the room this will hang in. This helps me with shading and color."

"Mom's in Miami. She lives in one of those old high rises. She came over from Cuba during the Mariel boat lift. She was pregnant with me and barely got her feet on the sand before I was born."

"So you are an American." Sofia smiled.

"I am but barely." They laughed, instantly bonding over the struggle of poor women to make it in America. In one comment Sofia and Rainy knew what Aleesha had faced and the scars she carried.

"I'm still working on it." Sofia offered more coffee.

"Where are you from?"

"Dominica." Rainy gave Sofia the side glance to tell her to shut up.

"Okay, let's talk about the colors in the room you think your Mom will hang this."

They went on to discuss the way her Mom had decorated the room and the colors she used. Then Rainy made a preliminary sketch and took a few pictures. They arranged to meet again in two days. Aleesha seemed to want to linger but Rainy had another appointment so she left.

"Damn, Sofia. Did you forget that woman's a cop? You ain't got no real papers, ya know?"

"I know, I know. I fucked up. Shouldn't told her that stuff. She just got to me, ya know?"

"Hey, its all right. That girl may be a cop but she's hurting. Probably the same story as us 'cept she got educated."

Aleesha had filled in her supervisor that Rainy was doing her portrait so she would have the chance to get more information. She was instructed to be casual but try to find out anything she could about Harvey Hall aka Roger Bannister.

Over the next few sessions Rainy turned the sketch into a very good likeness of Aleesha. She didn't give up much so the only thing to report was that the artwork was first rate and apparently was how Rainy made her money. Other than a late model car, there was no evidence of hidden riches and the living conditions on the houseboat were quite modest. What Aleesha did not report was that she was powerfully attracted to Rainy. She really didn't want her to be arrested and so far there seemed to be no reason to.

Quite a few wealthy women were willing to pay large sums to have their portraits painted. The houseboat studio soon became inadequate and Rainy began to look for a building to convert.

Chapter 44

Wilbur Bonnet wasn't sleeping well. He was still struggling with the knowledge that he was withholding evidence in the Harvey Hall investigation. His rationalization was that the people that had lost money had moved on with their lives. He also felt he had never been paid much by the town and deserved more. He had tracked down Harvey Hall after all so the case could be closed. He didn't want to admit that there was a lot of luck and very little police work involved. He knew it was a weak argument but he really wanted to keep the money and move to Key West.

He sat in the meetings of JITF and listened to the details as the FBI supervisor reported on the undercover agent's observation of Rainy. He saw the agent's picture and knew her cover name.

Agent Morales reported that Rainy's last name was O'Ryan and she was originally from Ireland by way of West Virginia. She had some past offenses such as prostitution, assault and minor fraud but really nothing that warranted much attention. Bank records on her were non-existent. She lived hand to mouth from the hustles she worked. Now she was making some money with her art which appeared legitimate. So it didn't look like she had any of the money Harvey stole.

One other remaining question was about the Catch 'Em. Where was it? It was possible that Rainy and her two friends or accomplices had stolen it. But that was hard to prove since no one was complaining that it was gone.

Barbara Frost Hall had not provided the task force with any new information. It seemed they were once again at the end of the trail. This time they did at least know that Harvey Hall, aka Roger Bannister, was dead. Wilbur recommended that each agency summarize what they knew in a final report and shut down the investigation for good.

The reporter from Nassau, Kyla had created a pretty thorough short documentary, 'Con Man Skewered!' but even it didn't shake loose any new information. The sketch of Rainy was noticed in Key West but that was about all. Most people who lived and worked in the Conch Republic kept to themselves and they certainly would not rat out one of their own.

It had been about three years since Barbara Frost Halls' shithead husband had run off and left her with nothing. However just in the last month things had turned around a little. She had gotten an off-the-books clerk job at the Quick Market. She was never going to be a country clubber again. At least she could help out with some of the bills in the house she now shared with her widowed cousin and their children.

One day she received an envelope from Visa forwarded from Harvey's old Frostville business address. She almost threw it away because she had never had a credit card and figured it was a junk mail solicitation. For some reason she opened it thinking that she just might apply for credit now that she was working. It was a notice stating that by prior agreement a card which was in her name as well as Harvey's was being charged $1800 for three years of rental at Secure Storage in Asheville, NC. She called the company and was told that a contract was on file that allowed the business to charge three years rent onto this particular card. The notice was for her files.

She was puzzled. She had never been to Asheville but immediately became suspicious because that is where Harvey said he was going when he disappeared.

She asked her cousin to watch her kids and drove her rattletrap car the two hundred or so miles south. She found the Secure Storage location and talked to a woman who owned the business. Once Barbara showed her identification the woman handed her the contract. It clearly made arrangements to pay three years rent and to renew automatically for unit 106. It was signed by Harvey Hall but had her name on it too.

Barbara found the unit. She saw the sturdy Yale lock and remembered the key she had found in the safety deposit box. Luckily she had dropped it in her purse. She fished it out. Her hands trembled as she worked the lock and slid up the door. She had no idea what to expect but was hoping it was full of money.

It was empty!

She sat on the concrete and cried. Of course. she had no idea that just a few feet away, Wilbur Bonnet had moved millions of dollars to the adjoining unit. It was as if her sociopathic husband had reached out from the bottom of the ocean and stuck it to her one more time.

Chapter 45

Rainy, Sofia and Higgs made a good team. All contributed to their lifestyle. Rainy's art was becoming increasingly popular and covered the reason she had money. With an attorney's help she even opened a bank account in the name of her company, 'Rainy Day Art, LLC'.

Sofia had become the sales and administration side of the operation. She was detail oriented and kept excellent records.She paid the quarterly income taxes as well as the other bills. Higgs was their resident handyman and could fix anything. His Mallory Square art was a great keepsake for the visiting tourists and his wild seafaring stories told in his unusual Spanish Wells accent were highly entertaining and profitable.

They were becoming fixtures in the community. People who had known Rainy and Sofia as part of the night trade conveniently acted as if they didn't. Some of those same people were now inviting them to fundraiser galas for all kinds of non profit organizations.

Key West has a long history of rogue turned philanthropist. It was one of the attractions of going to events and parties. The attendees were far more interesting because of how they had made their money. Generally, beside the usual professionals such as attorneys, doctors, business owners, artists and writers there might be strippers, transvestites, street entertainers, hookers, porn shop owners, politicians or smugglers.

Rainy negotiated a reasonable rent for the top floor of a well located building in Old Town. They set up a studio and gallery. The historic building had a nice size balcony which was perfect for art show entertaining. Conveniently, on the first floor was an attorney who was helpful with many business decisions.

Sofia had become instrumental in figuring out how to filter the buried cash into their legitimate bank account. Instead of hiding and running, the friends now were establishing their legitimacy. 'Rainy Day Art' became a must see stop for tourists and integral to the social swirl of Key West.

Rainy got more involved in the community and began to support other local artists and to give money to women's organizations.

Chapter 46

As the lead investigator in the Harvey Hall case Wilbur Bonnet assembled the reports from the various agencies and presented them to the Frostville Police Chief. The conclusion was that Harvey Hall was dead and money he had stolen remained missing or had been spent. There were a few news articles and Kyla's documentary aired nationwide. Soon Harvey Hall was relegated to the closed case file.

Wilbur sold his house and any belongings that he wouldn't need in a tropical climate. He packed his car and told his friends he was headed to Key West. Which he did with a detour to Asheville. At Secure Storage he retrieved one of the cases and made arrangements to pay three years rent for unit 108.

Wilbur figured he wasn't officially a felon until he actually spent some of the stolen money. He wrestled with his decision over the fifteen hour drive to Key West.

He had enough of his own money to start living in paradise. So he found a small furnished condo to rent on Roosevelt Boulevard. He casually slid the attache case under the bed. Then he went out and bought a scooter and put a for sale sign on his car. He wanted a simple life in Paradise.

The JITF closed the file on Harvey Hall and disbanded. Each agency ceased investigating the details of Harvey Hall's life.

Aleesha Morales, the undercover FBI agent, continued to sit for the portrait that Rainy was painting. There was no official reason to continue. She just was attracted to Rainy and wanted to spend time around her.

Rainy became less suspicious because Aleesha was in her studio frequently.

"You've been in Key West for a while now. Still on vacation?" Rainy repositioned Aleesha's arm to be consistent with earlier sittings.

"No, I actually live here now. Just rented a condo over on Roosevelt."

"That big building across from the beach?"

"Yeah, not exactly what I want but it will do for now."

"You got a job?" Rainy tried not to smirk.

"Yeah, picking up some shifts at Slackers."

"Used to be one of my favorite bars." Rainy leaned across Aleesha to fix a stray hair.

"Used to be?"

"Seemed kinda rough the last time Sofia and I were up there."

"It can be."

"Don't those redneck conchs scare you? I mean, you are a pretty girl and not very big." Aleesha felt excited. She desperately wanted to be with Rainy.

"I can handle myself. You think I'm pretty?"

Rainy didn't want to lead her on. "Of course I think you're pretty. Don't those guys hit on you all the time?"

"Most are assholes. Not interested in men anyway."
Aleesha knew Rainy wasn't going to reciprocate. She obviously
was with Sofia but at least she would know how Aleesha felt.
"Come by tonight when I'm working and bring Sofia. Nobody
will hassle you."

"Hey we will. Still one of my favorite places to get away
from the tourons. Let me finish this sitting and I will probably
have something to show you in a few days."

So life took on a sort of Margaritaville existence for
Rainy, Sofia, Higgs, Wilbur and even Aleesha. They were
strangely tied together as the result of a sociopath's thievery and
death. They went about living their lives in paradise mostly
ignoring this connection.

Wilbur spotted Rainy often in the small town. Once,
while shopping in Fausto's she was in front of him in the
checkout lane. She was laughing and joking with the clerk. Her
tattoo was clearly visible. She had no reason to recognize him and
now he didn't care. Wilbur didn't know for sure but figured they
both had Harvey Hall money.

The portrait of Aleesha was finished and Rainy had a
small party in the studio to unveil it. A few local women came
and some commissioned Rainy to do them. Aleesha still came
around for coffee.

Rainy's hard scrabble life made her not trust this period
of bliss. She felt the universe kept score. She understood why
some cultures made sacrifices to gods. She thought maybe she
could avoid the return of bad times if she gave enough to do
good. Her life began to revolve around Sofia, her art and the

many non profit activities that are so prevalent in Key West. These charity organizations supported a female population that is undereducated, unskilled and uninsured. They are women just like her and Sofia. They are or had been dependent on men that could abuse them in any way with impunity. Women who couldn't go to authorities because of where they came from or what they had done to get here.

Sofia and Rainy grew closer. They were in an exclusive relationship though each got hit on daily. Their flirty personalities sometimes sent out the wrong message but neither wanted to deal with the drama of cheating.

They started going back to Slackers because Aleesha made it clear to the patrons to leave them alone. She was small and cute but could kick some ass when necessary. She proved this in her second shift when a local fisherman grabbed her butt. She reacted with her law enforcement training and the redneck woke up on his back with blood running out of a broken nose. The crowd was stunned but got the message. She was still powerfully attracted to Rainy but understood the situation and was content just to be a friend.

Wilbur discovered Slackers. He knew the pretty bartender was the FBI agent using the name Aleesha Morales and lived in the same building as he did.

Some evenings he was sitting at the bar when Rainy, Sofia and Higgs came in. Everyone in the place seemed to know them and made an effort to say hello. Aleesha took over drinks as soon as they commandeered their favorite round top table. Even Wilbur nodded and lifted a glass when he made eye contact with Rainy. She smiled back but he was sure she had no idea who he was and he didn't care.

Chapter 47

The El Conquistador had refueled at Marina Hemingway in Havana. Over the last year, the boat had become a minor celebrity in the 'Con Man Skewered!' documentary. Everywhere it docked people took pictures and asked the crew if the story was true.

Luis Abelar, the owner was pretty surprised when he heard how much money Harvey Hall, aka Roger Bannister, had stolen. He had hung out with the man in the bars on Bimini and Eleuthera, so Luis knew he was wealthy. Chasing big game fish was a rich man's sport. With Roger dead, he wanted Rainy. Of course if she had his money he wanted that too. He knew she wouldn't be hard to find. If she and Sofia had met in Key West, that is where they would go.

The run from Havana to Key West wouldn't take more than a day. The El Conquistador flew a Panamanian flag so the Cuban Coast Guard would let the big yacht pass. The American Coast Guard might want to board but Luis had nothing to hide. He had been in Key West many times without incident. Luis told his captain to make arrangements to stay at the Key West Westin Resort and Marina.

Rainy and Sofia would know his boat but the chances were good they would not even see it. There were many large yachts all along the waterfront. More than a year had passed since

Sofia left so if she was there it was unlikely she would be expecting him now.

He would have some of his crew find and observe Rainy and Sofia. He knew he had leverage if they were still together. He was the kind of man who just took what he wanted.

Chapter 48

"Really? A croquet tournament?" Sofia laughed. Higgs just shook his head.

"Yep, I entered us and bought a table." Rainy held up the tickets. "We can invite a few more friends too. It will be fun. A fundraiser for 'Womankind'."

"Yeah, I've heard of them. Its a health care center."

"Right. So this is their big yearly event. We have to dress in period costumes. Then eat good food, drink champagne and play croquet."

"Higgs ain't saying much." Sofia laughed.

"Just trying to figure out what friend to invite, I am." He smiled.

"Higgs you're okay. Always up for adventure."

"Yeah, but I have a question." Rainy raised an eyebrow. "What period?"

"Its a Great Gatsby theme. That's a book..

"So we beat on, boats against the current, borne back ceaselessly into the past." Higgs quoted Gatsby.

Rainy smiled. "Sorry Higgs, didn't mean to insult you."

He shook his head. "Ain't had no schooling but I do know how to read. Warn't much else to do on that damn island. Where do we find the costumes and such. Ain't much for shopping."

"Sofia and I will take care of that. So who do you guys want to invite?"

"Does it matter who they are? I mean, is this a country club kind of thing?" Sofia asked.

"Don't matter, just have to be willing to get into the spirit of the event."

"I know a couple what juggles. Met them at Mallory Square. Good people.

"Cool. Need at least one more."

"What about Aleesha?" Rainy asked.

"The cop?" Higgs asked.

"The bartender. If she's a cop she ain't done nothing to us."

"Hey, its your party."

Even by Key West standards, the sight of Rainy, Sofia and Higgs dressed in 1920's regalia and riding into town on scooters was unusual enough to turn a few heads. When they got to the Truman White House they joined the crowd of Gatsbyesque attendees. They were greeted by Harry and Bess Truman (lookalikes), Roaring Twenties music, period cars and a long expanse of green lawn festooned with white tents. Some of the elegant crowd milled around the bar and silent auction offerings. Others practiced their croquet shots before the official beginning of the tournament.

Rainy wore a long lacy white dress. She had high button shoes, white gloves, a marvelous hat and parasol. Sofia had on a flapper style short fringed dress and head band. Higgs was quite dapper in white shorts, white shoes, white shirt, white cap and long argyle socks. His socks were deemed 'too argyle' and he was fined $100 by the Arbitrix of Elegancia, who was a very popular county judge in real life. He gave up the money in good humor.

Aleesha also went the flapper route in a short revealing fringed dress. The white material against the dark skin of her very fit body attracted a lot of admiration.

Bounce and Mademoiselle Ooh-La-La, who were Higgs' juggler friends turned out to have participated in this event quite a few times before. They were thrilled to be Rainy's guests and were appropriately attired. The fun of the event was in the mix of the people and their delightfully irreverent attitude.

It was decided that Higgs and Sofia, Bounce and Oh La La would team up to play croquet. Rainy and Aleesha were content to sit in the shade, drink champagne and watch.

Higgs surprised everyone. It turns out that croquet was an island activity that was taken very seriously in Spanish Wells. During the warm up he gave Sofia helpful instructions. She was athletic and competitive.

When the practice round was over the teams took a break. Under the tent they relaxed in the shade.

"You guys might have a good chance to win this thing from what I see." Rainy said.

Bounce and Oh La La who were runners up a few years before pointed out the past winners. "Some of these people take this real serious and practice all year."

"Might otta just not win." Higgs said.

"Why?" Rainy asked.

"Think people might not take too kindly to 'outsiders' bustin up their party."

"Good point, plus this is a fundraiser. So just have fun."

Higgs' insight was spot on. He and Sofia made it through the early rounds pretty easily as did Bounce and Oh La La. They could tell that some of the old timers were grumbling about the newcomers being 'ringers'. So, without being too obvious they played poorly and lost.

Bounce and Oh La La were longtime locals so no one had trouble with them. Under the tent the friends enjoyed the shade, the music and champagne. They rooted loudly for their favorites.

Rainy had a dark thought when two sinister looking men wandered onto the tournament grounds. They didn't stay long but gave her the creeps because they seemed to pay a lot of attention to Sofia.

Bounce and Oh La La got to the finals but lost. Everyone had fun and a lot of money was raised for Womankind. It was a pretty successful step into the world of philanthropy for Rainy. She was pleased that her or rather Roger's money was going to a good cause.

Chapter 49

The El Conquistador was docked directly behind the Westin Hotel in the newest section of the marina. Unless you walked around the corner from Mallory Square you would not see it. So Higgs, Sofia and Rainy had no idea that Luis Abelard was in town.

The two crew who had spotted Sofia reported to Luis. He questioned them about whether they saw Rainy but since her costume covered her shoulder they weren't sure. They knew Sofia. There were only two dark skinned woman at the event so she was easy to spot. They were not able to follow her because they were on foot and she rode away on a scooter.

Now that Luis knew for certain that Sofia was in town, he had more of his crew go ashore to find out where she lived and worked. He knew Sofia would lead him to Rainy.

Quickly the crew confirmed that Luis was right. They saw Sofia soliciting business for Rainy Day Art and easily found the studio. Rainy's skepticism of bliss was about to be proven true.

Sofia looked up from the form she was filling out to book a tourist from Minnesota for a portrait sitting. A creepy shudder shook her core. Behind the smiling over done matron was the slimy scowl of Luis Abelard. Her first instinct was to run but she calmed herself and finished filling out the form. She smiled and gave the woman a copy. Her brain was jumping and again she had to concentrate to keep from running.

"Sofia, looking good chica." Luis oozed out a slick smile as he stepped up into her space.

"Go away Luis."

"Why you being so mean, after all I done for you?"

Sofia snorted with derision. "Luis, you done for me all right. Now just leave before I scream. You don't want trouble in this town."

"Oh, this your town? Some little street whore gonna get me in trouble? Who the fuck you think you are?" He slapped her.

The action caught Higgs' attention. He was about fifty feet away and in the middle of one of his seafaring stories. He was up in Luis' grill in about ten seconds.

"What the fuck do you want, asshole?" Higgs was short but powerfully built.

"You? I know you too. Think you gonna take my little chica?" Sofia was on the ground caressing her bruised face.

"She ain't your chica." Higgs chest bumped Luis. Quickly two of El Conquistador's crew who were nearby stepped up and one cold cocked Higgs from behind with a leather sap. He went down in a heap.

Luis turned back to Sofia. "You ever want to see you mama again?"

Sofia sniffled and looked at him feeling everything good in her life was about to be crushed. "Then get up. You're coming with me." Luis nodded to his crew. They picked Sofia up and roughly escorted her to the seawall where a Zodiac from the El Conquistador waited.

.

The commotion stirred up the Mallory Square tourists for a few minutes but no one called the police. Wilbur happened on the end of the incident and saw Luis Abelard getting into the Zodiac with Sofia. He helped Higgs up. Bounce came over and filled Higgs in.

"Man, the guys that slugged you, took Sofia. Want to call the cops?"

"Naw. Don't do that."

Wilbur overheard the exchange. He knew Luis.

Rainy was alone in the studio finishing a portrait. She often got lost in the work. She realized it was getting late because the natural light had faded. As she cleaned her brushes she was mildly concerned that Sofia had not showed up. She usually came to the studio just after the sunset celebration broke up. On rare occasions she would stop for a drink with Higgs. Then she would call to tell Rainy where to meet them. She tried Sofia's cell and it went straight to voicemail.

For about a half hour Rainy continued to clean her equipment. She was listening for steps on the stair case. Just as she was about to leave to ride her scooter to Mallory Square, she heard someone come in the door. She sighed with relief which turned to panic when Higgs stumbled in and collapsed.

Rainy lifted his head. He was conscious. She put a wet towel on his forehead. He mumbled but she could not understand him. She had a sick feeling in her gut. Her mind was reeling with dark scenarios. She was about to call 911 when his eyes came into focus.

"El Conquistador." Higgs spit out.

" What? Did you say El Conquistador?" Higgs nodded. "Luis? Luis did this?"

"Naw, not that pussy. His goons. Took Sofia, they did." He struggled to sit up.

"Luis, the guy that owns El Conquistador took Sofia right from Mallory Square?"

"Yeah, one of his crew busted me from behind. When I woke up, Bounce and some local guy was trying to help me, said Luis took Sofia off in a Zodiac."

"Shit! What do we do?"

Chapter 50

Sofia was terrified. She was locked in a state room on the El Conquistador. She knew Luis. He could and would take anything he wanted. She was surprised that he cared anything about her. She at first thought he was just pissed because she had left Eleuthera with Rainy before he had a chance to dump her. But as she thought more about it she knew that didn't make sense.

Sofia knew Luis could make her do almost anything because he threatened to kill her family back in Dominica and she had no legal standing in the US. It wasn't an idle threat. She sat trembling waiting for something to happen. Finally she heard someone at the door.

"Chica, you think you can run away from me? Take off those clothes." Luis demanded. "Want to see your body."

At first Sofia wouldn't move. She felt she was sliding right back to the life she had fought so hard to escape. Luis grabbed her and threw her against bulkhead. He slapped her and backhanded her. She crumbled to the deck.

She knew he could kill her. She slowly removed her t-shirt and shorts. She wore a brief bikini.

"That's my chica." Luis helped her up. "See I can be nice when you do what I want." He raped her.

Chapter 51

Wilbur Bonnet was a man of habit and routine. He had spent a career as a police officer in which these traits were an asset. When he first moved to Key West he reveled in the fact that he no longer had to make roll call or dress in uniform. He got up when he wanted and his uniform was shorts, a t-shirt and flip flops. He had the whole day to himself. At first this was wonderous. Everywhere he wandered on the tiny island he came across new things to see and new people to talk too.

It had been just over a year since he discovered Harvey Hall's stash of money and he had not yet spent any of it. His modest pension and savings were enough for him to live his simple life. He didn't expect to be bored though. He found his routine had become predictable. So when he saw the tail end of the confrontation in Mallory Square that left Higgs on the ground, he perked up. At first he was reluctant to get involved but after Higgs stumbled away he asked Bounce what happened.

"Not sure. Out of the corner of my eye I saw Higgs get into it with an older guy. Then these two big guys came up behind him and Higgs went down. Before I could get over here they dragged Sofia to the seawall and into a Zodiac."

"How bad was Higgs hurt?" Bounce knew Wilbur on a first name basis and knew he was friendly with Sofia and Rainy too.

"Think he's okay. He came to and staggered off to find Rainy."

"Should we call the cops?"

"Don't think so, Higgs mumbled something about how he would handle it."

Wilbur had been in Key West long enough to know that the cops were rarely called to handle a dispute. Most of the people here had no use for the law. A lot of them came to South Florida to escape some kind of trouble they were in so they preferred to keep a low profile. In this case he knew Luis Abelard because he had ridden to Eleuthera on the El Conquistador after Harvey Hall was killed by the fish. He figured he had snatched Sofia because he was the kind of wealthy prick that just used women and she was a possession to him.

"Think I'll ride up to Rainy's studio and see what's up." Wilbur said.

"Yeah, okay. I'm gonna put Sofia's and Higgs stuff over with mine so it don't disappear."

"Good idea." Wilbur left Mallory Square, found his scooter and quickly arrived at the parking lot beside Rainy Day Arts. He sat for a minute wondering what the heck he was doing. The cop blood in him just couldn't stand seeing a shithead like Luis abuse women. So he climbed the stairs to the studio with no idea what he was getting into.

Wilbur knocked on the door. Rainy shouted to come in. She was only mildly surprised when he came into the main studio. Higgs was now sitting in a chair.

"Oh hey Wilbur, I was half expecting Bounce. Did you see what happened?"

"Came up on the tail end of it. Saw that Luis guy dragging Sofia off and Higgs here was just coming too."

Rainy knew Wilbur as a local but didn't know his background. She was suspicious though because he knew Luis' name. "How do you know Luis?"

In his haste to be involved, Wilbur realized he had revealed more than he intended. Now he decided to just confess. "Look, I got no interest in ratting you guys out. I just know stuff 'cause I was there when Harvey or Roger as you knew him got killed. I took the video."

"No kidding, so you saw Roger get stabbed?"

Wilbur nodded. "Yeah, and I rode on the El Conquistador back to Eleuthera to fill in the Bahamas Defence Force. I know Luis was pissed when Sofia was gone. Kinda surprised that he would show up here though."

Higgs and Rainy looked at each other wondering how much more Wilbur knew. "So you just happened to live in Key West?"

"Naw, came here about a year or so ago. Retired."

"Retired from what?" Now Rainy was really suspicious.

"You ain't gonna like this but I was a cop."

"A fucking cop. Wait a minute! I saw you in Islamorada didn't I? You were packing your trunk and I picked up a can of shaving cream you dropped." Wilbur nodded at the memory. "What do you really want?"

Higgs got to his feet. He looked ready to throw Wilbur out of the studio.

"Look before you get mad let me fill you in on what I know."

Wilbur told Rainy and Higgs how he was staying in Islamorada on his retirement trip. He related how he just happened to be fishing on the Dawn Lee next to the El

Conquistador when Roger was stabbed by the marlin. He said he had video taped the whole thing. When the BDF came he volunteered to go back to Eleuthera to officially tell his story for the authorities. That was how he knew about Sofia and first heard Rainy's name. He admitted taking Roger's shaving kit and having it tested when no one could really prove who he was. He said he had been chasing Harvey Hall for years and was already suspicious that he and Roger were one and the same. He told them about the task force and how a FBI agent was assigned to find Rainy and report on her activity. Finally he said he had the case closed but he did not reveal that he had a stash of Harvey Hall's money.

Rainy and Higgs were a little stunned. They had gotten so used to their Key West lifestyle they had pretty much thought no one knew anything about how they got here.

"So, what? You've gotten to know us so you can have us arrested?" Rainy was incredulous.

"Naw, I don't care what you know about Harvey Hall, or Roger, as you knew him. I just came to Key West to retire."

"Why did you come here now?"

"Well, habit I guess. I am or was a cop my whole life. I know what kind of prick Luis is. It didn't sit right back in Eleuthera when he discovered Sofia was gone and acted like he owned her. Now, he has dragged her off. Ain't right."

"So can you help us get her back?"

"I can try. What do you think Luis wants? I mean beside Sofia? You think he came here just for her?"

Rainy shook her head. "Not sure". Deep in her gut she knew exactly what Luis wanted.

"Don't you think the police could help?"

218

"Look Wilbur...what's your last name?"

"Bonnet."

"Well. I appreciate that you want to help, but Sofia ain't got no papers and no official is gonna board Luis' boat just cause we say she's on it."

"I get it. What if I go aboard asking questions?"

"You got a badge and a gun?" Rainy asked.

Wilbur nodded.

"Does Luis know you're retired?"

He nodded again.

"There are at least ten crew on that boat." Higgs added.

"Yeah, that might be tough."

Rainy's cell phone rang. She hit the speaker function. "Oh my god. Sofia?"

"Ah the beautiful Rainy." Luis' sleaze oozed into the room.

"What do you want?" Rainy's voice turned cold.

"Why don't you come over to my boat. We can finish what we started back in Eleuthera?"

"Don't think that's gonna happen, you asshole."

Luis laughed. "See you know just what I like. If you want to see this little slut again you will come." Luis slapped Sofia and she cried out. "Hear that? I can play rough too. So come over. Oh, and bring two million of those American dollars you stole from Roger."

"Ain't gonna happen."

Another slap and whimper came through the phone.

"I'll call back."

"If you go on that boat with money he will just leave," said Wilbur. He had moved with Higgs and Rainy from the studio to the dock.

"Finish what? He said you could finish what you started in Eleuthera.?" Wilbur asked Rainy as they all stood looking at El Conquistador.

"Sofia got me to come onto that boat. She was gonna convince Luis to take me with them so I could get away from Roger. I did a little Dom shit on Luis and he ate it up. A lot of these rich yachty types like to be abused. I left before he got his rocks off so now he is all desperate to have me."

"So Wilbur, you know about Roger's money?" asked Rainy.

"Yeah, some of it he stole from me."

"But you ain't gonna turn me in?"

"Got no interest in that."

"Wilbur you are lying but right now I don't care, you might be the only one who can help."

"Well, maybe not the only one."

"Huh?"

"You know that pretty bartender at Slackers?" Wilbur asked.

"Aleesha?" Rainy looked over at Higgs.

"Yeah. She's more than a bartender."

"We figured," Rainy nodded.

"You did?"

"Yeah, we made her for a cop," Rainy revealed..

"How come you hang out with her?" Wilbur wanted to know.

"She ain't done nothing or I guess she ain't got nothin on me."

"I guess. She just reported on your activity." Wilbur said.

"See. Nothing much to report."

"Yeah. But she's FBI. She's trained. She might help." Wilbur stared up at the El Conquistador.

"Officially?" Wilbur shook his head.

"Probably not. Want to talk to her?" Rainy nodded and they all headed to Slackers.

Chapter 52

It was early evening and Slackers was slammed. There was no designated 'Happy Hour'. The locals who drank here stopped by on their way home from work. The crowd thinned around dinner time then picked back up when the hard core drinkers came back.

Even though she had her arm deep in the beer cooler when Rainy came in, Aleesha noticed her right away. She grabbed a can of beer and slid it down to a sunburnt fisherman. She turned and made a couple of Mojitos which were Rainy and Sofia's usual first drinks.

"Where's Sofia?" Aleesha placed the two drinks on the table in front of Rainy, Higgs and a regular she knew as Wilbur. He came in frequently and they both lived in the same condo building.

"That's what we came here to talk to you about." Rainy took a sip of the mojito.

"Okay give me a few minutes, the rush is almost over. You guys want something?"

"Beer's good for me." Higgs said and Wilbur nodded.

Aleesha brought two beers over to the high top table and climbed up on a bar stool. "So what's up? You guys look kinda serious. Everything okay?"

"Look Aleesha, I'm just gonna say it." Rainy took a gulp of her drink. "We know you're a cop and we need your help." She whispered because she didn't want to blow Aleesha's cover.

"Uh huh. My shift's almost over. I'll meet you at your studio." Aleesha went back behind the bar.

"Let's finish our drinks and go."

"Think she'll show?" Wilbur asked.

"Yeah, she will," Rainy said.

"By herself?"

Rainy shrugged. "We'll see."

Rainy opened the door of the Rainy Day Art Gallery for Aleesha. "The guys are in the back." She flipped the closed/open sign so they wouldn't be disturbed.

Aleesha walked down the hallway to the kitchen. Higgs and Wilbur were sitting at the small table. They were now drinking coffee. Rainy pulled up two more chairs.

"So why do you guys think I'm a cop?" Aleesha asked.

"Well, we kind of made you about a year ago." Rainy smiled.

"Yeah?"

"I saw you a little too often and then you signed up for a portrait."

"Hey, its a small town and you do good work."

"Yeah but you dressed like a cop and most young women don't care about having a portrait done. We figured you were checking up on us or at least me 'cause of Roger." Rainy poured herself a cup of coffee.

"Roger?"

"Come on Aleesha, we know. Plus Wilbur here confirmed it. He's a cop too."

Now Aleesha was surprised. "What?"

"Wilbur Bonnet's my name. I was the Chief in Frostville, North Carolina before I retired. Your supervisor sent your reports to me."

"So you know the file on Rainy is closed?"

"Yeah, I closed it." Wilbur said.

"Okay we know I'm a cop. FBI actually, but I'm working on cases that don't concern any of you. So why am I here?"

"Did you get any information about a guy who owns the El Conquistador?"

Aleesha nodded. "Abelard, Luis. Drug dealer, human trafficker. Owner of that boat, the one Roger or as we now know Harvey Hall was on when he was killed."

"Yeah that's right. I was on the Dawn Lee that was fishing near them and took the video." Wilbur sipped his coffee.

"Uh huh. Most of this is public record."

"Look Aleesha. What you may not know is that Sofia came to Eleuthera on the El Conquistador." Rainy explained. "She left with me and now Luis Abelard has kidnapped her."

"The El Conquistador is here? He took Sofia? When?"

"Couple of hours ago. He called from her cell phone and wants me to come on board." Rainy was getting upset.

"Why?"

"Well, he's into S&M and I know about that stuff."

"We know he's a drug dealer and trafficker. He would risk a kidnapping charge for rough sex?" Aleesha wanted to be incredulous but she couldn't because she knew too much about the dark side of people.

"He knows I won't go to the cops, 'cause Sofia is illegal."

Aleesha and Wilbur looked at each other. "Well hell he was wrong."

"He also wants two million dollars." That statement sucked the air out of the room.

"Luis Abelard has Sofia on his boat. He is using her to get to you because he wants to have rough sex? Do I have this right?" Aleesha asked.

"Pretty much except he also wants two million dollars."

"You may not want to answer this. Do you have that much? Is it the money Harvey Hall stole? Before you answer let me say I'm your friend but if you have that money I can't let that slide." Aleesha was not going to jeopardize her career for Rainy.

"If it was money I made from selling 'Catch 'Em' would that make a difference?"

"You mean the boat you stole from Harvey Hall."

"No the boat Roger gave me."

Aleesha knew Rainy was lying. "So he gave you the boat and you sold it for two million dollars?"

"Not that much but with what I have made in the last year I can come up with about half of what Luis wants."

Aleesha knew this was not likely, but she wanted to be on Rainy's side. "So why give him anything?"

Rainy looked pained. "If I don't go on that boat with cash he'll kill Sofia."

"If you go on that boat he'll kill you both."

Wilbur looked at Rainy and said, "I've been involved in hostage situations. If you give in to demands it almost always ends badly. Right now he has Sofia. I don't mean to be cruel but so what?" Rainy looked like she had been punched.

"I get that you love her and you two are a couple but what does Abelard know? I would advise blowing him off. Tell him if he comes ashore in Key West you and your friends will kick his ass. Be hard core. I was on his boat, he might have been a feared drug dealer in his day but now he's old and must be running out of cash 'cause this is stupid."

Aleesha was nodding in agreement. She had been trained in hostage negotiation and while she had not actually handled a case she knew Wilbur was right

"So what? Ignore the guy?" Rainy asked.

"Yeah, pretty much. When he calls again, tell him to fuck off and hang up or better yet don't answer at all."

"Yeah if you don't answer it will really confuse him." Wilbur scratched his chin. "Being unpredictable might give us a break."

Aleesha said. "If you don't answer, he'll have to find another way to communicate. That might give us a chance to get on board."

"He'll kill her." Rainy's eyes teared up.

"He won't do it in US waters. Too risky. Why kill her anyway?"

"Just that Dominican drug lord shit. If I don't show up with the money he'll have to do something brutal."

"Yeah but it still won't get what he wants."

"It will if I get on the boat."

"That solves nothing. Gets both of you killed."

"What if I just give him the money?"

"A better idea but doubt he'll give Sofia back. He's just gonna take the money and leave."

"Wreck his boat." Higgs had been quiet until now.

"What?" Rainy turned to him.

"Just fuck up his boat."

"How?"

"Mess up the props, mess up the engines, mess up the fuel. Lots of ways."

Wilbur scratched his chin again. "Aren't you gonna have to get on board?"

"Maybe not. Can dive under and fuck up the shaft."

"Won't he be watching for something like that?"

Higgs shrugged. "Better'n nothing. Shit could just ram him."

"That I like." Rainy perked up. "With what?"

"Can buy a heavy old tub and just pin his ass to the dock. Cause all kinds of shit. Fire maybe. Would have the Coasties all over it. Maybe an opening to get to Sofia."

"Damn Higgs, I like the way you think." Wilbur grinned.

"I'm not officially hearing any of this, but I like it." Aleesha smiled.

"So when Luis calls what do I do?" Rainy started pacing around the kitchen.

"Now, I think you probably should answer and stall. Tell him you need time to get the money together. That way Higgs can find a way to disable El Conquistador."

Aleesha agreed. "Yeah, lead him on. Make him believe you will come on board when you have the money. But Higgs, I have a question."

"About what?"

"Won't the marina have a security guard or two?"

"Yeah but they won't even be looking at the water. Mostly they're just rent-a-cops that keep tourists away from them yachts."

"What about El Conquistador's crew?"

"Yeah, might cause some shit. I'm gonna find a boat and a crew."

"A crew?" Wilbur asked.

"Know some guys." Higgs went out of the door.

Chapter 53

Luis Abelard had half of his crew on lookout for anything suspicious happening near the El Conquistador. He had done shake downs before and knew anything could happen. So his two Zodiacs were patrolling around the marina. Rainy didn't worry him but Higgs did. Higgs was a tough waterman from Eleuthera. He wasn't sure of the connection to Sofia but if he worked for Rainy he could be a problem. He still wanted a dominatrix session with Rainy but the money was more important. Luis wanted to do this deal quickly and get away from Key West.

Rainy's cell phone rang. It was Sofia's number. She looked at Wilbur and Aleesha. "Answer it?" They nodded.

"I want you and the money here now." Luis said.

"Ain't got the money. Need more time."

"How much more time?"

"Gotta get it wired. Can't do too much at a time, you know that. So it'll take at least another day."

"If you're stalling, I'll kill her."

"One more day and I'll have it."

"Bring it over tomorrow at sundown, we'll have a little party." He laughed and hung up.

"Okay, now what?" Rainy asked.

"Have to see what Higgs comes up with." Said Aleesha.

Most resort towns have an unseen population. Well, unseen may be the wrong word. They are seen but consciously ignored by the tourists and are a source of constant irritation for business owners and homeowners. Key West has its share of homeless wanderers. They are attracted to the year round warm weather. They shelter in the mangroves, in park gazebos, on the beach, in abandoned boats, empty vacation properties, the library and in fast food restaurants. Some get in trouble, most ghost around trying to live day to day.

Higgs had befriended quite a few of these men. He brought them food and more importantly hung out and listened to their stories. He had a certain affinity with down and out people because he had been there. So when he needed a crew for this crazy mission he knew just who to go to. He figured he could do it with one more guy who knew boats. He found Mike drinking coffee in the Mcdonald's on Roosevelt. He used to be a merchant mariner and now survived doing a few gardening jobs.

"Hey Mike." Higgs sat at his table.

Mike nodded. "Ya know the mangoes are bigger this year?" His deeply lined permanently tanned face lit up.

"Didn't know that." Mike just grinned and took one out of his bag and cut it up. "Taste that."

Higgs enjoyed the sweet orangey, peachy flavor. "Good Mike, it is. Say can you help me with something?"

"You got it."

Higgs and Mike prowled around Stock Island for several hours looking for a heavy wooden boat. What they found fit the bill. Sitting at the end of finger pier was a 45' Carolina deadrise. The specs on the for sale sign said she was twenty one gross tons, twin diesel engines recently rebuilt and had basic electronics. She had an 18' beam and 6' draft. She was forty years old but the yard attendant said she ran pretty good. The price was $48,500.

"Gonna take up commercial fishing again?" Mike asked Higgs.

"Kinda, look can you wait here? Poke around and see what equipment she has. I'll be back directly."

Higgs rode his scooter back to the gallery. He found Rainy nervously pacing around in the kitchen. Wilbur and Aleesha were down at the dock keeping watch on the El Conquistador.

"Glad to see you. Find anything?"

"Yeah, gonna need some cash."

"How much?"

"Owner wants $48,500. Plus there are some dock fees and need fuel. Probably fifty would do it."

"Okay...got that much over at the houseboat. Luis gave me until sundown tomorrow to come up with the two million."

"Not gonna give it to him are ya?"

She shrugged. "Can you have the boat ready to ram him by then?'

"Yeah."

"Need to get Wilbur and Aleesha and figure this thing out."

The captain of the El Conquistador had just fired up the engines when Luis came onto the bridge.

"I've arranged to keep the slip while we're gone. Plan to come back tomorrow just before sundown." Luis gave instructions to head out to sea. He didn't want to be docked overnight because it made the boat easy to board. He felt Higgs might try.

Aleesha called Rainy to tell her the boat was leaving.

"What?" Rainy was worried.

"Don't panic, I think he's just moving away from the dock so he won't be boarded. He'll come back to get you and the money."

"I guess." Rainy replied. "Look, meet me and Higgs at my houseboat. We gotta plan this."

Aleesha and Wilbur found Rainy on the upper deck of the house boat.

"Where's Higgs?" Wilbur sat in one of the deck chairs.

"He just left with some money to buy a boat."

"What did he find?"

"It's a big old wooden boat."

"Should do the trick." Wilbur again scratched his chin. "I guess we should figure out exactly what the trick is though."

"Yeah, you know this Abelard character is gonna be wary as hell. We need to think about contingencies." Aleesha said.

"Like what?" Rainy was nervous.

"Well he might bring the El Conquistador back to the dock or he might send in a Zodiac to pick up you and the money. We need to be prepared for either."

Aleesha's phone chirped. "Look I've got to deal with this, I'll be back as soon as I can." She left.

"Is Higgs gonna move the boat over here?"

"I didn't ask him. But that's a good idea. I'll see if we can dock it next to us. How about you call him and see what he plans to do." Rainy went to talk to the marina manager and Wilbur got Higgs on his cell phone.

They agreed that it was a good idea to bring the boat into the Garrison Bight marina to be closer to where they anticipated the El Conquistador would dock. Higgs told Wilbur he had help so he would be there as soon as he could.

Rainy came back up to the deck of the houseboat. "The manager said we could tie up next to us for a few days but then we would need to find another marina."

"Good. Higgs said he would be over here as soon as he could."

"Can he move that big a boat by himself?"

"He said he had help?"

"Not surprised. Old Higgs has made a lot of friends here."

"So have you." Wilbur looked at Rainy. "We could put together an army if you want to. Just raid that big ass yacht."

"Damn Wilbur, you're getting all Rambo. Rather keep this thing under control."

"I know you're right but just once I'd like to really take down the bad guys."

Rainy smiled. "We'll get 'em."

Higgs climbed up to the pilot house and started up the engines. When the diesels were warmed up he gave Mike a thumbs up and he pulled in the stern and bow lines. The old boat was pretty rough looking but moved smoothly away from the dock. The faded name on the transom was 'Albatross, Key West'.

The marina manager who handled the sale said the boat was abandoned in the Bahamas after the owner mysteriously disappeared. The current owner salvaged and rebuilt her but tired of the project. So Higgs was able to knock the price down to $40,000 cash for a salvage title and no questions asked. Higgs felt a strange connection to the boat that he couldn't explain.

Mike finished securing Higgs' scooter on the deck then joined him in the wheelhouse. "The day is ours." He declared. "I know this boat."

"You do?" Higgs wasn't sure how many cylinders Mike was firing on but he did know his way around boats.

"Ah yes, the master of this vessel was one Victor Hugo Bustado. A scholarly sailor and damn fine cook."

Higgs smiled. "What happened to him?"

"The good die young." Mike stared up at the sky.

By scooter it would take fifteen minutes or less to get from Stock Island to Garrison Bight. The Albatross made a top end of about nine knots and would have to make the twenty plus mile trip all the way around Key West. Since Higgs knew the draft was 6', he planned to follow the charts and stay in the channel. No short cuts.

"Hey Mike take the wheel. Just keep her in the deep water." Higgs pointed to the depth finder. "Going below."

As he climbed down from the pilot house, Higgs watched Mike. He could see that while the old guy was kind of mystical, he knew how to handle a boat.

Down in the engine room Higgs was pleased to find the engines humming and no water in the bilge. It was the first time since they docked the Catch 'Em in Islamorada that he had been back at sea. He wasn't sure if he felt nostalgia or nausea. Then he shook himself and remembered he had an important mission. Rainy and Sofia had been good to him and now he had a chance to repay them.

Chapter 54

On the El Conquistador, Sofia was left to cower in the corner of the state room where she had been locked up. Luis had repeatedly raped her which she could block out. Fearing she would never see Rainy again though was driving her crazy. Now she could feel the boat moving and worried she would be dumped at sea.

Luis' ferret-like face appeared when he unlocked the door. "Time to air you out, kinda got a stink. Get down to the shower and then come out on deck." He turned and left.

Sofia edged out of the cabin and down the corridor to the guest head. The hot shower helped revive her a bit. She knew she could deal with Luis' clumsy fucking. She just worried he would kill her.

She found a bikini among the clothes she had left behind when she fled with Rainy. Out on deck she could see the boat was well out at sea. No chance for help.

"Ah chica, can see why your lover will pay for you. She got the hots and plenty of jack. I'm gonna show her what a Dominican man can do. She gonna want to never leave." He grabbed his crotch and laughed. He was dressed in his favorite, personally designed admiral uniform. Sofia wanted to belittle his sexual prowess but knew such a comment would mean another bruise or worse.

"Yeah honey, she gonna love it. Why you gotta go through all this shit? Rainy would come on board to get some of that." She caressed Luis and purred into his ear.

"You ain't forgot, huh?"

"No baby, I ain't." Sofia knew how to play Luis. She just needed to stay alive until she found out his next move.

The El Conquistador was cruising in an East / West track off of Key West. Luis had instructed his captain to stay well offshore but be ready to come back to the dock by sundown the next day.

Higgs was piloting the Albatross in the same general vicinity as he circumnavigated the island. Rainy had called him to let him know that Luis moved his boat. They figured he had gone out to sea just to avoid being boarded at the dock. So Higgs knew both boats could be near each other. It occurred to him he could stage an emergency and call a 'Mayday'. If El Conquistador was close she would have to respond. It was the law of the sea that any nearby boat will help a stricken vessel. It might be a chance to get on board and find Sofia. Of course, Luis Abelard would probably ignore any maritime law since he ignored international law all the time.

Higgs could see two huge cruise ships. He realized one or both would respond to a 'Mayday' so that little plan would not work. There was a lot of boat traffic because Key West was such a popular port of call. El Conquistador was not close enough for Higgs to see so he decided to continue on to the marina in Garrison Bight.

Wilbur helped Rainy prepare dock lines and fenders to secure the boat. They waited on the top deck of the houseboat so they could see Higgs when he entered the Bight.

"Is this a crazy idea Wilbur?" Rainy was worried.

"Yeah, but the thing about crazy is that we might catch them off guard. I doubt Luis will expect to be rammed. Just might cause enough chaos to let me slip on board."

"What about me? I've been on El Conquistador." Rainy got up from the deck chair and paced around.

"Yeah but I have too, so I pretty much know the layout. If Luis sees you, who knows what he might do."

"But Luis knows you too. In fact he knows all of us except Aleesha."

"Yeah, but we can't expect her to help. She may want to but she will screw up her career doing some kind of rogue cop thing."

"Well it might not be totally rogue." Aleesha had climbed up to the deck and overheard the conversation. "If I just happen to be in the vicinity when some crazy shit happens, I can choose to respond."

"Look there, coming down the Bight." Rainy pointed.

Higgs brought the boat closer in order to raft up. The houseboat crew climbed down to handle the lines. When he swung the boat around to line up bow to bow, Rainy saw the name on the transom.

"Albatross!! Oh my god, this is Hugo's boat!"

"That it is." Replied Mike who was handling the stern line. "A fine man he was." He snugged the boat against the fenders.

Higgs turned off the engines and climbed down from the wheelhouse. "Come on over. She's old but solid, she is."

Rainy, Wilbur and Aleesha stepped over from the houseboat. "This is Mike." Higgs said as he coiled a stray line. "He said he would help us."

"Mike, I know you." Rainy said.

"That you do fair lady." Mike did a little bow.

"You used to come over here when Hugo did his cookouts."

"That I did, every Friday."

"So who was this Hugo?" Higgs looked at Rainy.

"We are living in his old houseboat. He was a Key West fixture. His Father used to drink and carouse with Hemingway. Hugo was a salvage diver in his younger days and plenty wild too. He and this guy Freddy who you say killed your brother were always treasure hunting."

"So Hugo and Freddy came over to Eleuthera looking for treasure?"

"Well more specifically gold. Some guy who was murdered in the forties was supposed to have had a shit load. Freddy and Hugo were obsessed with finding it." Rainy explained.

"Yeah somehow my brother got all tangled up in that and got his self kilt, he did." Higgs looked agitated. "This boat must be where it happened. It's why I felt a weird numbness when I boarded her. She's a death boat."

Higgs and Mike rolled the scooter off the Albatross and up the pier to the parking lot. "Mike, you can stay on the boat tonight. I'm gonna get some food."

Mike joined Wilbur, Rainy and Aleesha on the houseboat deck.

"Where's Higgs?" Asked Rainy.

"Went off to find sustenance." Mike had a vocabulary that was more akin to an English professor than a homeless guy.

"So you've agreed to help us?"

"That I have. A damsel in distress is a saintly mission."

"Don't know how saintly it's gonna be if someone starts shooting." Wilbur looked at this motley crew and wondered if they could pull this rescue off. "Aleesha, how do you think this should go down?"

"Since I'm not officially part of any of this, I think I will just position myself in Mallory Square. That fits with some of the undercover work I'm doing. So, if shit happens it will just be a coincidence that I was near.

"What kind of shit will happen?"

"Hey, let's eat this food." Higgs had climbed up to the deck with bags of Dion's chicken. "I can tell you what might happen."

"Ah, the feast before battle." Mike dug in.

They all laughed. "At least one of us is not worried." Rainy poured sweet tea from a jug and passed the cups around. "No alcohol tonight."

"Okay, so the El Conquistador will have to be in the same slip as she was yesterday because that is the only one big enough. There's plenty of room for me to get up some speed in the channel and turn into marina." Higgs took a bite of chicken.

"Ramming speed, as it were." Mike chuckled.

"Yeah, ramming speed. If I hit right at the stern the blow will damage the shaft and propeller. Maybe blow up a fuel tank."

Now Rainy was more concerned. "If El Conquistador blows up it might kill Sofia."

"So, when Abelard calls back. Make sure he knows you have to see Sofia before you will bring him the cash. Make sure she is near the bow. If a tank blows at the stern she should be safe."

"Should be?"

"Yeah, but you guys need to be ready to board." Higgs looked at Wilbur and Aleesha. "Guns and all."

"Won't they have weapons?"

"Guaranteed. One of the reasons I will then be officially involved." Aleesha explained. "As soon as I see a weapon, I will call for back up."

"Back up?"

"Yeah, just so happens a buddy of mine is here on vacation."

"Just so happens?"

Aleesha grinned. "Uh huh, we went through the Academy together. She gets it."

"Well, there's gonna be chaos. So I think I should be the one to grab Sofia." Wilbur said. The others nodded in agreement. "And one more thing, nothing will go as planned." Rainy looked worried. "This ain't the movies. We will surprise 'em but not totally. Luis will expect something. We just need to be ready for anything and move fast." Wilbur was fired up.

"What happens when the local cops and Coast Guard show up?" Asked Rainy.

"Let's just worry about saving Sofia." Wilbur was in full cop mode.

"Yes, save our fair damsel and ride back to Camelot." Mike toasted everyone with his cup of tea.

Chapter 55

The El Conquistador had moved into water shallow enough to hold an anchor but away from the main channel and boat traffic. The captain posted a bow and stern watch.

"Nobody can approach without us seeing them."

"See that the lookouts stay awake." Luis barked. He was wired and wanted this deal done. He left the flybridge and went to his cabin.

Sofia was again locked in a guest cabin. She could tell the boat was at anchor. She wondered if she could swim to safety. Maybe get to another boat or an island. There was no porthole in the guest cabin. She banged on the door until a crewman opened it.

"Gotta pee." She brushed by him to get to the head. Through the porthole she could see a slip of land but no buildings, docks or boats. Just another barren sand bar. When she emerged from the head, the crewman steered her back to the guest cabin. He pushed her inside and closed the door.

She didn't hear the lock click. When she turned the knob the door opened. The crewman had forgotten to turn the lock. She knew the guys that Luis hired to run his boat were just street goons and not very bright. She crept through the corridor and out onto the deck.

The night was very dark. There was no light from the surrounding environment. Sofia knew she could just slip over the side of the boat and not be seen. She could tell there was no where to swim to except the small sand bar. Also, she knew sharks fed at night.

She stood looking out over the dark water. She felt hopeless. She did not want to slide back into Luis' demented world where she was just a fuck toy. She knew that if Rainy came on the El Conquistador neither of them would survive. She decided that if she killed herself at least Rainy wouldn't have to undergo the humiliation of belonging to Luis.

She saw the crewman smoking in a deck chair. She ghosted by him, climbed over the stern into the water.

She thought she would just sink to the bottom and be enveloped in the warm tropical womb. The water wasn't very deep and when she hit the bottom her natural reflex was to kick upward. When she surfaced she swam to the sandbar.

Luis couldn't sleep. He called the bridge and told the mate to bring Sofia to his cabin. He knew she could ease his tension. After fifteen minutes Luis was in a rage. Sofia had not shown up.

Luis put on a robe and went out into the corridor. The first mate was hurrying toward him.

"She's gone! Cabin is empty!"

"How? Who helped her?" The mate shrugged. Sensing trouble, Luis ducked back into his cabin and got a weapon.

Then he and the the first mate went on deck to find all the lights on and the crew lowering a Zodiac.

"Did you search the boat? Why do you think she went overboard? Where could she go?" Luis was fuming.

"Half the crew is searching here. The others going out to that sandbar." A mate pointed off the starboard side of the El Conquistador.

Luis went to the rail. "Point the spotlights over there." He shouted up to the bridge.

The big powerful lights swung over to the small sand bar. There didn't seem to be any vegetation or structure for Sofia to hide behind. "Nothing there. Go over anyway."

Sofia was laying flat in the sand when the searchlight swept over her. She couldn't tell if she was seen, but judging by the commotion on deck she knew it wouldn't take them long to find her.

When the light passed her again she crawled back into the water. She removed the bright yellow bikini and let it float away. Her copper skin blended into the dark water. The light came back across her but didn't hesitate. Now what? When the sun came up she would be seen right away.

As the Zodiac headed toward the sand bar, she swam back to the boat staying low in the water. The retractable swim platform was down to allow access for the Zodiac. She just held on and kept to the shadows. She could hear Luis barking commands and the on board crew running all over the boat. Once they had searched everywhere and on the sand bar maybe they would think she drowned. If she could just stay out of sight she might be able to climb on board and hide.

She began to shiver even though the tropical water temperature was in the eighties. She was about to climb out and onto the platform when she heard the whine of the Zodiac's engine. She ducked as low as she could as the rubber boat came alongside. One of the crew was waving her yellow bikini top.

Luis ranted and threatened the crew. He was determined to find out how Sofia got out of the cabin and apparently drowned. The crew goon that failed to lock the door did not confess but Luis figured it out.

"You dumb ass mother fucker! Do you know how much you cost me?" Luis shoved a silver plated, pearl handled .45 automatic in the sniveling man's chest. Then he walked him to the deck rail and fired the gun. The first shot flipped the man into the water. Luis leaned over and unloaded the clip. Sofia flinched with each shot.

The sharks moved in and churned the water into a red foam.

"I want that bitches body." Luis reloaded and shot at the frenzied fish. The first mate gave orders to keep searching.

Sofia had to climb out of the water and onto the swim platform. She was naked and shaking, from fear and near hypothermia. Her movement was caught by the Zodiac crew.

"She's there!" One of them pointed.

Luis rushed to the stern and looked over the transom. Sofia was crouched on the swim platform. She was thinking about jumping back into the water but the vicious thrashing of the sharks made her hesitate. It was one thing to drown. Quite another to be torn apart.

"You ain't gonna want to do that." Luis sneered. "Get your ass up here."

Chapter 56

Rainy worried about Sofia all night. She was ragged and stressed in the morning. When she stumbled to the galley she found Higgs and Wilbur already up and drinking coffee.

"Did anybody sleep?" She poured herself a large mug and sat .

"Not much. This whole thing makes me nervous." Wilbur scratched his chin. Higgs nodded.

"We got a long day ahead of us. What else should we be thinking about?"

"Kinda want to take the Albatross out the channel and see if the El Conquistador's nearby."

"What good would that do?"

"Just think I would like to get my eyes on that boat. Ya know?"

"Yeah I do." Wilbur said. "Just might be an easier way to get on board without a bunch of shit."

"Like how?" Rainy asked.

"Not sure. But what if Luis sends a Zodiac to pick up you and the money, or something. Maybe he even comes ashore and we could grab him."

"Not likely. But I get that you want to be in a standby position." Wilbur stood and stretched.

"No, not what I want. I say we ram the fucker where ever we can. Not wait until sundown." Higgs was pretty worked up. "Just not let him set the play."

"Some value in that. Surprise usually shakes things up."

"But won't he just start shooting? Won't it be a surprise to ram him in the marina?" Rainy was worried about Sofia being used as a shield.

"Yeah, just antsy. Hate to sit here and wait."

"But if Luis spots you on the Albatross he'll just take off. Right now, seems to me the best plan is to pin him in the boat slip."

"Yeah, okay. Just hope he comes back to that same slip."

"Hey, can't we find out if that slip is reserved?"

"Well I would think so. Just call and request a slip for our boat and see what is open. The radio on Albatross work?"

Higgs nodded. "Yeah, I'll go do that."

"A reservation for the slip don't mean that Luis will come back." Rainy worried.

"Yeah, but the lady what took my call was sure it was reserved for El Conquistador."

"She gave that up?"

"Yeah after I said we was fishing together in the Hemingway Tournament" said Higgs.

"Okay that's something. Maybe."

"Look this might not be helpful but I been thinking on it. Mike and me can round up some more guys."

"To do what?" Now Wilbur looked interested.

"Figured the more men we rush onto the boat, the more of a shitstorm it'll be." Higgs explained.

"Yeah and the more people might get hurt."

"Don't matter." Mike had come up from the Albatross.

"What do you mean it don't matter?"

"Shit, guys I know'll go through a wall to help that Sofia."

"Huh?"

"Yeah, y'all don't know but she helps all of us. Gives us food, money, helps us with government stuff. Just is nice and smiles. Knows our names. I could come up with five guys easy, maybe ten."

Rainy, Wilbur and Higgs looked stunned. "She knows your names?"

"You betcha. Nice to be recognized. Gives a man respect. These guys are vets, they know how to go to war.

"Well, hell we got us an army. Mike, go round 'em up. We'll get some food cooking." Wilbur said.

"Right, an army marches on its stomach."

Chapter 57

Sofia was dragged off the swim platform and thrown back into the guest cabin. She was too exhausted to fight and crawled between the sheets of the bunk. She fell into a fitful sleep.

Luis posted a guard in the room. "She kills herself or gets away, feed your ass to the sharks." He waved the .45 in the terrified man's face.

Out on deck, Luis lit a cigar and looked over the rail. There were no signs of the sharks or the dead crewman in the dark water. He had no remorse. In fact he was pleased to have re-enforced with his crew why he was the boss. Now that he had his bargaining chip back he looked forward to having Rainy and her money.

An unintended consequence of Sofia's unsuccessful escape attempt was that Luis now was feeling pretty cocky and his crew was terrified. He had not killed anybody in a long time but he liked how powerful it made him feel. He wasn't worried at all that Rainy might try something crazy. He planned to cruise back into Key West and have a little sun down party. He finished his $400 Cohiba and went to his cabin to get some sleep.

Chapter 58

Mike brought five more men to the marina. He helped them park their shopping carts that held all of their belongings on the afterdeck of the houseboat. He led them up to the top deck where Rainy, Higgs and Wilbur were cooking up some hamburgers and laying out the fixings.

"Might as well call us the 'Dirty Half Dozen'. Mike laughed as the guys helped themselves to the food.

"Y'all eat up." Rainy smiled. She had seen most of these guys around. She pulled Mike aside. "What did you tell them?"

"Just informed them that our favorite friend needed help. Didn't take much. These are men of honor. Maybe a bit dusty and forsaken, but men of honor none the less."

"Do they know that whatever happens could be dangerous?"

"Battle hardened, they are. 'March into hell for a heavenly cause'."

Rainy's eyes filled with tears. She realized these men were forgotten heroes.

Everyone moved down to the afterdeck to plan the rescue.

"So my thinking is that we let the El Conquistador tie up. It will be bow in and right next to the wharf. That's the only slip big enough. We have about half of us on Albartross and the other half on the dock. Since I have a weapon and so does Aleesha we split up. That way we can come from two directions after the ramming." Wilbur suggested.

"Not a bad idea." Aleesha had joined the group.

"This is Aleesha, she's gonna help." She nodded to a couple of the men. They all knew her from Slackers. Most of them knew she was in law enforcement too.

"I will be on the dock doing my official work, if they start shooting we'll have them pinched."

"Yeah, about the shooting?" Rainy looked at Higgs. "These guys..."

Mike interrupted. "These men can handle it. They will fight."

"Hey I appreciate their spirit but what are they gonna fight with?" Wilbur stood with his hands upturned. "Just having this many guys to rush the boat will throw off the crew but I'm worried that someone will get shot."

"Someone will get shot if El Conquistador fires first. We will respond with a classic broadside. Boys, show 'em"

The 'dirty half dozen' each reached into his shopping cart and withdrew a weapon. The armament ranged from a .38 police special to a sawed off twelve gauge shotgun.

"Jesus, I don't want to know anything about this." Aleesha laughed. "This is a god damned army."

"So, what if half the guys hang out with their carts on the dock near the boat slip and the rest act like deckhands on the Albatross?" Higgs suggested.

"Maybe just a couple of cart guys on the dock, you know how they attract cops." Wilbur said. "Everyone else on the Albatross."

"I think that is as good a plan as any. Do we wait till Luis contacts Rainy?" Aleesha asked.

"Yeah, then she can demand to see Sofia on the bow."

"That can be my signal to ram El Conquistador."

"You guys all right with this?" Rainy asked the vets. They all nodded.

"We should have an exit strategy." Wilbur looked at the group. "The best outcome would be to get Sofia and everybody onto the Albatross and back out of the marina. If El Conquistador is damaged enough it won't be able to follow."

"So what happens if the Albatross is too fucked up to move?" Rainy asked.

"Plan B should be to get Sofia off El Conquistador and over to the dock. Then to my car." Aleesha said. "I can park it at the entrance to Mallory Square because it is an official government vehicle. Then you guys scatter."

"Thinking if we can cut El Conquistador's mooring lines, should be able to push her sideways in the slip. That would do the most damage and not mess up Albatross too much." Higgs explained. "Any of you guys got a big knife?"

One of the 'Dirty Half Dozen' smiled. "I'll take care of them lines." He pulled a machete out of his cart.

"Okay, I'm glad you guys are on our side." Aleesha chuckled. "This is so illegal I won't even try to justify it."

"Sometimes in the course of history men have to march into the breach." Mike put his hand over his heart.

"Okay General Mike, let's get ready. Whoever is on the dock be looking for me. As soon as I see Sofia on the bow, I will turn into the slip." Higgs punched his left hand with his right. "They won't know what hit 'em."

Chapter 59

Luis had the captain of the El Conquistador weigh anchor and start towards the marina. He was feeling pretty invincible and horny. Now he wanted Rainy and her money. He rounded up his crew to yell at them.

"You dumb fucks need to hear this. Anyone gets on board without my permission? It's your ass." He waved his silver plated .45 in their faces. "We tie up. Nobody goes ashore. Got it?" He left the salon and went back to the flybridge.

The crew were street goons recruited by Luis to work on his boat. They mostly put up with his tantrums and fancy uniforms because it was an easy life. Now they were grumbling. They had seen one of their own killed and they knew Luis had the only guns. Most were thinking about jumping ship. No one said anything though because they didn't know who might rat them out.

The Westin Marina has less than forty slips and a fairly small turning basin. The captain of the El Conquistador carefully maneuvered the Prestige 750 into the slip by the wharf. With the bow pointed toward the resort, this was a pretty big mistake. If Luis wanted to leave in a hurry he would have to turn around. He was on the bridge and didn't say anything. He was confident that he was in control and didn't think Rainy could do anything outrageous.

"Post watches, nobody goes ashore." He told the captain. "Have someone make sure that slut, Sofia, is cleaned up and keep an eye on her." Then he went to his cabin to rest in anticipation of his sexual tryst with Rainy.

The captain of the El Conquistador was the only professional sailor on the boat. He put up with Luis' eccentricities because he was paid twice the going rate for a boat this size. Now that he had seen the murder of a crewman, he knew it was time to leave.

Three of the vets and Mike stayed on the Albatross with Higgs. The other two guys pushed their carts to Mallory Square which adjoined the Westin Marina. Rainy waited in her art studio just up the street for Luis to call.

Aleesha parked her car near the walkway to the dock. She could see that the El Conquistador was already there and tied up where they expected. She called Rainy and Wilbur to let them know.

"Okay Rainy, all we need is for you to see Sofia on the bow. I am sitting on a bench just past the gangway. The cart guys are not far away. You might have to show yourself to get Abelard to put Sofia on the bow."

"I'm gonna stay in my studio until he calls. Then I'll let Wilbur know. When you see Sofia, be ready."

Wilbur climbed up to the pilot house of the Albatross. "Aleesha called. The El Conquistador is in the marina."

Higgs started the engines on the Albatross. His crew handled the lines. They motored slowly out of the Bite.

255

Every day tourists made the pilgrimage to Mallory Square to watch the sun go down. The channel in front of the square also fills with tourists on day sailing boats of all sizes. The boat traffic made good cover as Higgs slowly moved the Albatross into position. With so many vessels jockeying for position to see the sunset, no one on El Conquistador paid any attention to the old wooden boat.

The crew of the El Conquistador was nervous. They didn't really know what Luis was up to. He would not let them in on his plot to extort money from Rainy. He didn't trust them and knew they only respected fear. Most had figured out that Sofia was involved. They had never seen Luis so angry as when he thought she had gotten away or drowned. Killing their crewmate had set them all on edge. Now they figured some kind of exchange was to take place.

The vets were anxious too but for different reasons from the El Conquistador crew. They were ready for action. They wanted to feel useful. To them the El Conquistador was Hill 41 in Vietnam. Saving Sofia was their mission. Men with nothing to lose could be very dangerous.

"You got the money, sweet thing?" Luis' slimy voice slithered out of Rainy's phone.

"Yeah."

"Bring it."

"Not giving it to you till I see Sofia standing on the bow."

"Easy enough, bring it bitch. Bring it now."

Rainy hung up thinking, *I'm gonna bring it, you asshole!*

She called Aleesha and Wilbur. She put two beach bags full of cut up paper in the trunk of her Malibu and drove to the Westin. There she commandeered a baggage cart and pushed the 'luggage' to the dock.

"Come on you little slut. Time to earn me some money." Luis pushed Sofia who was in shorts and a t-shirt out of the salon onto the deck.

"You, put the gangway down." He barked at two of the crew as the pushed Sofia toward the bow.

"Rainy, you got it?" Luis shouted. Not wanting to use the word money in such a public place.

"Right on this cart." Rainy pushed it closer to the boat.

"Bring it down to the gangway." Luis lifted his shirt so she could see his gun. "No funny shit."

Higgs and Wilbur were watching the El Conquistador and the marina with binoculars.

"I see Rainy on the dock and there is Luis and Sofia on the bow. Machete guy just chopped the stern line."

Higgs turned the Albatross toward the the marina opening in the sea wall and pushed down both throttles. "Hang on!" He shouted from the pilot house. The old boat came up on plane with her bow high out of the water as the diesels churned.

Some of the tourists on the wharf saw the boat gaining speed. They saw the rough looking crew and figured it must be part of the show. Some bunch of fake pirates raiding the island.

257

The Albatross rammed the El Conquistador. The crunch of wood on fiberglass and the loud spinning of the twin props got the attention of hundreds of tourists, vendors and street performers.

Higgs had hit on the back left corner of the El Conquistador's stern and just dug in. He pushed the 75' boat against the pilings on the starboard side. He could tell he had done some serious damage to the big boat's props and fuel tanks. He could smell fuel leaking but there was no immediate explosion.

Wilbur and the men on the Albatross jumped to the El Conquistador. On board the crew were picking themselves up off the deck. Most of them threw up their hands when Wilbur showed his gun. General Mike had to subdue one with a punch to the face and two more jumped overboard.

Sofia and Luis had also been thrown down on the deck.

"You bitch!" Luis got up and pointed his gun at Rainy. "Bring that money now!" The vet with the cart nearest the bow pulled his weapon. Luis shot him. The Vet fired his shotgun as he fell but missed. Luis grabbed a dazed Sofia and edged backward using her as a shield.

Luis saw that what was left of his crew were surrounded by some kind of tough looking gang. He could tell the El Conquistador was heavily damaged from being rammed by a big old boat. He dragged Sofia toward the salon.

"Federal officer! Drop the gun!" Aleesha shouted from the wharf. She had her gun pointed at Luis. He looked over at her with disdain and fired a shot which missed but hit a tourist.

Wilbur had climbed to the flying bridge where the captain gave up immediately. He had a clear shot at Luis and took it. The bullet hit Luis in the shoulder.

Sofia felt Luis' grip go limp. She turned and ran toward the gangway which was dangling off of the boat. Rainy had rushed to the side of El Conquistador.

"Jump! You can make it." Sofia did and landed in Rainy's arms.

"Go!" Aleesha yelled. "Get out of here!"

Luis made it into the salon. He had fought many drug wars and wasn't about to give up.

The chaos on the wharf after the shots was epic. Tourists were screaming and running in all directions. Sirens were getting closer.

Wilbur came off the flying bridge. He told the vets on the deck to scatter. They quickly jumped to the wharf and disappeared into the mass of people.

"You guys got about one minute to get off this boat or deal with Luis' mess." He told the captain and remaining crew of El Conquistador.

Wilbur ran to the stern and jumped over to the Albatross. Higgs calmly put her in reverse. He backed off the El Conquistador and out of the marina. The Albatross quickly got lost in the boat traffic that was edging in to get a closer look at what happened. Smoke curled out from the El Conquistador's engine room.

Aleesha knelt beside the woman that took the bullet meant for her. It had grazed her upper left arm.

"Think you are gonna be okay." She reassured her. "I'm a federal officer. Help is on the way." Aleesha used her phone to call in the EMTs and her fellow officer for backup. She was now officially engaged. She knew things were going to get complicated.

Chapter 60

"I thought I would never see you again." Sofia was shaking and crying in Rainy's arms.

"You are safe now." They were in the art studio. Rainy gently laid Sofia on the couch. "Just rest, I gotta find my phone." She dug around in her shoulder bag and pulled it out. "Need to find out if Higgs and the guys are okay."

"Yeah, I recognized those guys."

"Sofia's Army. They all volunteered to rescue you."

Sofia's eyes teared up. "Hope they are safe. That Luis is one brutal bastard."

Rainy hit her speed dial for Higgs.

"Everyone okay?"

"One down. We are heading back to the houseboat. Most of the guys scattered. Not sure what happened to Luis. Wilbur says he shot him, he did."

"Yeah, saw that but Luis made it into the salon. Guess we'll have to see if Aleesha and the cops go for him. Who got hit?"

"Not sure. It ain't gonna be pretty. How's Sofia?"

"She's sitting right here. Think we'll lay low for now."

"Good idea. Gonna tie the Albatross up and me and Wilbur are gonna go to Slackers."

"Well that's a good idea. If Sofia's up for it we'll meet you there."

"Okay." Rainy ended the call.

"One of the guys got hit?"

"Yeah, he got shot by Luis. Don't know how he's doing."

"Want to go to Slackers? Meet up with Wilbur and Higgs?"

"Yeah, can I borrow some flip flops?"

When Wilbur and Higgs climbed up to Slackers. Everyone was looking at the smoke coming from the marina. The buzz was about a boat being rammed and now it was on fire.

"All kinds of shit went down." One excited bar fly was saying.

"Were you there?" Wilbur asked.

"Yeah man, down at the Square hustling. Saw this old piece of shit wooden boat ram all up on this shiny plastic yacht."

"What happened?"

"Hard to know. Heard gunfire though. That's when everybody started running. God damn! Got my ass out of there."

Wilbur got a couple of beers and he and Higgs moved away from the crowd to a round top table by the stairs. They could just see the El Conquistador's superstructure through the smoke.

"Hope the god damn thing burns the fuck up." Sofia draped her arms around Wilbur and Higgs. "You guys saved my life." She hugged them. Rainy did too.

"Want a mojito?" Higgs asked and the two women found it hysterical. They were still laughing when he came back to the table with the drinks.

"General Mike!" Rainy ran to hug him as he came into the bar. "Who got hit?"

"It was Jerry. The old coot's fine. Took one in the hand."

"The hand? I saw him hit the ground." Rainy said.

"Not surprised. Probably hurt like hell. Got a shot off though. A warrior never falters. Now the General would like a libation."

"Drinks on me." Rainy told the bartender.

"For everyone?" She asked.

"Right! Till we're knee walkin."

Now all the patrons lost interest in the boat fire and turned to do some serious drinkin'.

One by one Sofia's Army found their way up to Slackers. Each was hugged and added a little more to the growing story.

Seems that the boat didn't blow up but did catch fire. Luis decided to fight and shot at the arriving cops and firemen. That earned him a visit by the Swat Team and the Coast Guard. The boat was still burning but no shots were now being fired.

At the point where Sofia's Army and the whole Slackers crew were about incoherent, Aleesha and her friend Ashley showed up.

They were royally welcomed. Since Aleesha worked part time at Slackers her presence took the celebration to whole new level.

Amid the alcohol induced revelry, Aleesha revealed that her superiors were satisfied that she had a tip that Luis Abelard was trafficking in drugs and women. She didn't admit to being part of Sofia's Army but none of her bosses cared. There would still be many reports and much to sort out.

The door to the bar banged opened and Jerry stumbled in. His left hand was bandaged but he was ambulatory. Sofia's Army burst into cheers. The rest of the patrons joined in suspecting that these guys had something to do with the events in the marina.

Epilogue

Aleesha Morales was promoted for taking down a notorious drug lord and human trafficker. She and her friend Ashley live together in Miami. They visit Key West often and always enjoy the fun that swirls around Rainy.

Higgs made peace with the spirit of the Albatross. He knew his brother died on the boat but he felt he was honoring him by bringing her back to life. He even started fishing again.

Wilbur found the mission he needed. He formalized 'Sofia's Army' into a non-profit. He and General Mike help Veterans who need to be rescued from the demons of alcohol and drugs.

Rainy and Sofia were married in a beautiful ceremony at the West Martello Tower garden gazebo in Key West. It was attended by hundreds of friends. They continue to support women in need.

The El Conquistador burned to the water line. Luis Abelard died from gunshots and the fire. An anonymous donor provided the money to have the hulk moved out of the marina and added to an offshore reef.

Barbara Frost Hall is still a clerk in a convenience store in Virginia.

Harvey Hall's stolen money is still buried in five gallon Home Depot buckets near the bat tower on lower Sugarloaf Key. Some remains in multiple silver attache cases in a storage unit in Asheville, NC.

None of the money has been returned to the people of Frostville, North Carolina, yet.

Have you read?

Hemingway's Heist

"I bought this book yesterday...thinking that I would read it over the next week or so when I had time. I haven't been able to put it down and just finished reading the whole book. It kept me wanting more and more and kept me constantly trying to figure out the next twist and turn.
Chuck Ball is a Master with words and I look forward to reading more of his books!"

Best Regards,
Allison

Mingo's Cave

"I have only been to the islands a couple times. This book was such an easy read. I took such pleasure in reading it because I could relate to places, etc. I like the drama, romance and mystery. I can't wait for Chucks next book. I highly recommend this book because I am not much of a reader but this book has changed my entire perspective so much that I bought my very first kindle. Thank you Chuck."

Judy

33138864R00150

Made in the USA
Middletown, DE
02 July 2016